Brother of The Struggle

a novel by

Jason Goudlock

Dedicated to the loving memory
of James and Bernice Boozer

ACKNOWLEDGEMENTS

To my Brother, James: Thank you for reconnecting our brotherly ties, as well as beautifully raising my nieces and nephew, Brianna, Zoey, Christina, Jessica, and Brandon.

To William Nichols: Without you the completion of *Brother of The Struggle* may have never been realized. Thank you for your years of support. Your words of encouragement gave me the confidence to overcome many obstacles.

To Nicia Aiyetoro: Thank you for helping me realize I had the ability to become a writer, as well as all for the days you spent typing the early drafts of *Brother of The Struggle*.

To Siddique Abdullah Hasan: Thank you for all of your constructive criticism and brotherly advice--especially when I didn't want to hear it. You showed me by example how to stay focused on my goals and priorities.

To Jason D: Thank you for being a friend, as well as the best webmaster in the world.

Brothers and Sisters of the Struggle Recognition: Robert Jones; Ezekiel Marcell McCarroll; Tramell Paterson; Jermaine Watkins; William "Sneeze" Johnson; Jerry Smiley; Cleveland Boxing Legends: Ray "The Rainman" Austin; Anthony "Amp" McGhee, and Donald Ray Williams; Norman Whiteside; Michael Wright; Mario Redding; Jerome Brown; Percey Jones; Charles Nickleberry; Bomani Shakur; Gregory Curry; Kunta Kenyatta; Jonathan "Zilla" Williams; Brandon Harris; Will and

Ashante Smith; Melvin King; Sabrina Cooper; David ClarkKamiesha Toland; Shean K. Grey; Carmen Dews; Jadelene Gordon; Cleveland's Antwone Fisher; Shante Worthy; Mike Dixon; Terry Little; Christopher "Hound" Smith; Kevin Anthony Pope; Alphonse Brown; Mike Tyson; "Rashid" Johnson@Rashidmod.com; Robert Keith and Lila Jackson; Ricardo Francisco; Jaan Laaman@4strugglemag.org; Mikesean Woodland; Prentiss Williams; Sean Swain; The coalition of FREEOHIOMOVEMENT.org; Teri Woods; Crystal Sweeney; Robert A. Richardson of Pagescape Press; Colin Kaepernick; and LeBron James (for being so that just mentioning your name in a letter has changed my life!)

To Filmmaker Samuel Crow: Thank you for caring about my situation of injustice and using your filmmaking talent to make a documentary about it. Because of you, people all over the world will know more about some of the dark realities of mass incarceration in the United States.

Introduction

In February of 1994 Jason Goudlock went to prison at the age of eighteen. He had drawn a six-to-25 year sentence for assault and robbery and a mandatory nine-year "firearm specification." He was not a model prisoner, to put it mildly, but even so, reading soon became an important part of his incarceration despite his anger and rebellion, and he wrote to me about how that happened:

> *At the very beginning of my incarceration I got into a fight and went to the hole (May or June of 1994), and, as a result, I started reading newspapers and books that the older guys would give me to keep me occupied. I remember I didn't adjust too well to being in the hole, and I used to try to get on the officers' nerves by banging on my cell door and flooding the range. I didn't know it at the time, but my disruptive behavior was interfering with the older guys' attempts to convey contraband into the hole. So, their solution was to keep me occupied with material to read.*

One of the books he read was *The Life and Times of Frederick Douglass* (1881), and Douglass's account of his escape from slavery and his work for abolition gave Goudlock the idea of writing his own story. When he had finished about 200 pages of an autobiography and was feeling good about his progress, he got into another fight and was put in the hole again. When he was able to return to his cell, the manuscript was gone. He gave up on writing for several years and devoted much of his energy to arguing and fighting with other prisoners. In 2005, he was charged with assaulting an officer although Goudlock's legs were fastened in irons and his hands were cuffed behind him at the time of the alleged attack. He was transferred to the Ohio State Penitentiary (OSP), the "supermax," in Youngstown, where men often called "the worst of the worst" are kept in isolation.

At first Goudlock responded badly to solitary confinement, shouting obscenities at correction officers. His grim sense of solitary confinement is apparent in *Brother of The Struggle* when the protagonist, Malcolm Xavier Jordan, encounters the hole:

> It was my first time in the hole, and the chaotic environment wasn't anything like the cellblocks, where you could sometimes find a little peace and quiet. Unlike those fully enclosed steel and concrete cells, the cells in the hole had old-fashioned see-through iron bars that let anybody see into your cell. And the hole was dirty as hell. The tiers smelled like the back of a garbage truck and were littered with stains of dried up feces that inmates threw at each other or at officers. This kind of biohazard warfare, called "bombing," happened so often the prison officials didn't bother to clean it up.

In the OSP Goudlock also came under the influence of fellow prisoner Siddique Abdullah Hasan, an African-American imam, who was sentenced to death following a 1993 prison uprising at the Southern Ohio Correctional Facility in Lucasville, Ohio. Hasan played a crucial role in negotiating an end to the violence in Lucasville, and other inmates were given shortened sentences for testifying against him. (See Staughton Lynd, *The Untold Story of a Prison Uprising*, 2011.) Hasan's cell in the supermax was nearby, and when he was exercising in a dayroom in front of Goudlock's cell, they began to talk. Goudlock says the imam told him, "You don't have to meet every situation with aggression. It's like when a bug keeps flying in your face: you don't have to *kill* it. All you have to do is just swat it away." It took a while, but Goudlock began to listen, and he read some of Hasan's essays. Although he wasn't drawn to Hasan's religious vision, he seems to have been influenced by the imam's emphasis on the potentially healing power of communication. Before long, he stopped shouting and began to write again.

This time he decided to write a novel based on his experience growing up in Cleveland and landing in prison. He started working on it during the summer of 2005, writing late at night when his cellblock was quiet. Shortly after he began writing the book that would become *Brother of The Struggle*, Goudlock heard from a woman, Nicia Aiyetoro, who offered writing advice and agreed to type his manuscript. But isolation worked on Goudlock. He started to shout again, to argue relentlessly with men on his cellblock, and he stopped writing. Disappointed, Aiyetoro finally lost patience, and in 2008 she stopped corresponding with Goudlock.

In June of 2008 I received a letter from Goudlock, who had read an essay of mine about isolation and torture that appeared on the website PrisonerSolidarity.org. He introduced himself, mentioned the essay, and told me he had an idea for a documentary film about the challenges he expected to face when he was released from prison. In our sixth exchange of letters, he finally mentioned his novel, and I volunteered to help him complete it.

There were interruptions in the months and years that followed. Goudlock was repeatedly denied parole, and he struggled with anger and depression. He was moved to a cellblock where three white supremacists tried unsuccessfully to attack him while he was in the shower. Then he was shifted out of the Ohio's "supermax" and into the Toledo Correctional Institution. As he learned to live among other prisoners again, he became increasingly concerned about the effects of a change in Ohio law that causes problems for "old-law" inmates sentenced, as he was, before July 1, 1996. The new sentencing guidelines reduce periods of incarceration and don't require inmates other than convicted murderers to go before the Parole Board. But the new guidelines don't apply to "old-law" inmates. Most importantly for Goudlock when he moved out of isolation, the 1996 law created a growing class of inmates able to pick fights with "old-law" inmates without risking changes in their own sentencing status. The "old-law" inmates, on the other hand, are likely to be denied parole for fighting. Goudlock, who has been denied parole five times, has now served more than twenty years for a first conviction for robbery and assault, and he has become a crusader against the injustice caused by Ohio's new sentencing guidelines.

The "old-law" injustice at the heart of essays Goudlock has written for his website, FreeJasonGoudlock.org, figures in *Brother of The Struggle*. (Goudlock's website was developed for him by an Ohio volunteer prison reformer.) The novel's protagonist, Malcolm Jordan, describes a newspaper article he finds when he comes out of the hole at the age of 21. The article, "Sentencing Reform Could Free Thousands," tells about a law that establishes new sentencing guidelines for inmates who committed their crimes after July 1, 1996. These "new-law" prisoners never have to go before a parole board empowered to judge whether they are fully enough rehabilitated to be released. They serve, instead, the sentence imposed by the judge in the court where they are tried. The article points to a "potentially messy legal dilemma" because the law is not retroactive, and Jordan recognizes the problem immediately. He says: "Messy legal dilemma didn't get it. The thought of having to serve five or more times longer on my prison sentence than somebody coming in under the new guidelines made my blood boil! In a span of just a few seconds I saw images of prison rebellion flashing through my mind."

The problem Jordan recognizes in the article is the dilemma Goudlock has lived with increasingly. And his dilemma as an "old-law" prisoner leads him now to embrace isolation for reasons it has taken me years to understand.

When Goudlock first wrote to me in the summer of 2008 after finding my essay, he was held in isolation at OSP, the state's "supermax," where he spent at last 23 hours every day alone in a small cell. Neither isolation nor reading was new to Goudlock. Since he went to prison at eighteen, he had often been in the hole, and beginning when he was twelve, he lived almost three years at a private residential treatment community in Pennsylvania that provides the basis for an important setting in the novel, a place where he spent two-thirds of his time in isolation and often read from encyclopedias stored in a room where he was kept. In the essay, "Contemplating Torture," I mentioned that Alexis de Tocqueville and Gustave de Beaumont reported in *The Penitentiary System in the United States* (1833) that "absolute solitude, if nothing interrupt it, is beyond the strength of man; it destroys the criminal without intermission and without pity; it does not reform, it kills." I speculated that our country's acceptance of the increasing use of isolation in our prisons, beginning in the early 1980's, might have prepared us for the Bush administration's attempt to "define cruelty down" as a way of justifying our use of torture in the "war on terror." I had a sense Goudlock agreed with me.

But over the years, Goudlock came to believe he was safer and better able to read and think and write in isolation. Entering prison at the age when many people go off to college, he has come to value solitude and the habit of thought sometimes called "deep attention." Here is how he put it when I reminded him of the psychological costs of solitary confinement, as well as the parole board's inevitably negative take on his preference for solitude: "Trying to study and write in a general population cell makes as much sense as a student trying to study for an exam at a heavy-metal concert instead of in a library. Solitary confinement is no library, but it is the lesser of two evils."

Still, Goudlock chooses isolation at considerable sacrifice. He must give up his "mini-tablet," which gives him access to music and limited email. In 2013, the year before he completed *Brother of The Struggle*, Goudlock began to write relentless criticism of Ohio's prison system on FreeJasonGoudlock.org., and in 2014 the Ohio Parole Board imposed on Goudlock the harshest penalty they had at their disposal, a five-year extension of his sentence. He understands the five-year extension as punishment for his preference for life in the hole as well as his criticism of the criminal justice system.

Even as I've slowly come to accept Goudlock's reasons for preferring the hole to life in the general population I continue to remind him about the risks and losses, and I recently added that calling out the criminal justice system for racism, as he often does, is also dangerous. "The most powerful man in our country," I said, "President Barack Obama, has found it difficult to talk about that issue without getting criticized for 'playing the race card.'"

Goudlock responded: "How can a broken criminal justice system ever be fixed if people are unwilling to voice the truth? And besides, when it comes to fighting for justice as an incarcerated black man or woman, we must be fearless and fierce because the long history of racism in the United States reveals that the deck is stacked against us. Our country still has a very, very long way to go before it actually becomes the country of 'liberty and justice for all.'"

Despite interruptions and crushing disappointments when he was denied parole, as well as hours spent crusading for the rights of "old-law" prisoners, Goudlock pushed on with *Brother of The Struggle*, and I have wondered why the so much of his energy and hope seemed focused on writing this fiction. He knew an autobiography or memoir based on his experience would be more likely to sell, and Goudlock has the tactical temperament of an entrepreneur. My best guess is that by creating Malcolm Xavier Jordan, the protagonist of *Brother of The Struggle*, Goudlock protects himself from the overwhelming disappointment that might paralyze him if his work were stolen or trashed again before he could find readers. At least the loss would not be his own life story, as though he had been executed. This fragile protection and the historic echoes of Malcolm X in his protagonist's name perhaps allow him to confront the crimes and injustice that have shaped his life, as well as the miraculous hope he has somehow salvaged from more than two decades of incarceration. *Brother of The Struggle* is a powerful story of improbable hope born in isolation.

Brother of The Struggle

Chapter One

Silence engulfed the occupants of the prison transport van as it traveled up the long driveway towards its destination, the Logan Correctional Facility in Woodhill, Ohio, a rural town with a population of 2,200 in northeastern Ohio, forty-five minutes away from the city of Cleveland.

Seven or eight inmates, including me, were being transferred to the LCF prison from the Cuyahoga County Jail, but I paid them hardly any attention. It was winter, early February 1994, and it was freezing inside the transport van. All I could think about was the cold and prison. The combination of cold and nerves, not knowing what to expect of prison life, had me paralyzed.

I'm over six feet, and I weighed about 180 pounds then, none of it fat, so I wasn't afraid so much of being targeted by a bully. Being Black also helped to calm my nerves a little because the way I heard it, it was the White boys who got extorted and sized up to be somebody's subservient penitentiary housewife. *They* were the "fresh meat" the macho penitentiary homosexuals drooled over, the ones who would hear, "shit on my dick or bleed on my knife." It was the White boys who would take a stripping, not me. But all that reasoning didn't help much. I was nervous as hell.

I was an 18-year-old first offender, convicted of "complicity to commit robbery" on multiple counts along with two "drug-related offenses" and a charge of "carrying a concealed weapon" -- and was sentenced to four-to-15 years. On top of that I didn't have any family outside of my mother, and she was a drug addict. I'd never even seen a picture of my father. Going to prison felt like being pushed out of an airplane into the Amazon River with nothing to grab onto.

Chapter Two

I entered the world March 13, 1975, three months early, with some serious complications. I suffered from jaundice and pneumonia. If this was any indication of the trials and tribulations I would be confronted with throughout the course of my life, then ultimately I would be fine because I pulled through to the delight of my proud mother, Angela Marie Jordan. She named me Malcolm Xavier Jordan and chose my first and middle name to remember and honor the late, great humans rights leader, Malcolm X. Although the X in Malcolm X's name didn't stand for Xavier, as mine did, my mother chose the name so when I wrote it out the way she taught me before I entered pre-school, it would read *Malcolm X. Jordan.*

Whether she knew it or not, the given name linking me to the revered, controversial, assassinated statesman would be a gift and a curse—more gift than curse.

In the spring of 1982 my mother and I were living in a three-story, run-down building in the infamous Morris Black Projects on the east side of Cleveland. We stayed on the second floor, in a one-bedroom, one-bathroom efficiency infested with roaches. Surprisingly, we didn't have rats or mice. My mother worked as a secretary for a health insurance company at $9.00 an hour, which was a decent wage in the early '80's. So we had some money coming in. It kept clothes on our backs and food on the table.

On the days my mother worked she would wake me up at 5:30 a.m. so I could eat breakfast and have time to walk to school. She had to catch the RTA bus at 7:00, and she got me a baby-sitter so I wouldn't have to walk through the projects by myself. Every morning after breakfast my mother took the ten-minute walk with me to the baby-sitter, and even though I hated getting up so early, I understood even then that she was only being overly protective of me out of genuine love. She loved me, and I loved her back.

When I was seven, my mother was 27. She was smart, and she had skin the color of butterscotch with long, dark hair. When I looked into my mother's hazel brown eyes, it was as if I'd been put into some kind of hypnotic trance. I couldn't stop looking at the splendor of her deep, penetrating, almond-shaped eyes. When she suspected me of telling a lie, she would make me look her in her eyes. I couldn't get a lie past that stare, an intuitive glare like a lie-detector test. In addition to her beautiful eyes she had a flawless complexion. She was six feet with a lean, athletic physique, and she could have been a model or a movie star if she'd had the desire.

One evening I was sitting in the living room watching something on TV when I noticed my mother was going back and forth between the bedroom and the bathroom. This had happened before, I realized, and I *never* heard the toilet flush although I heard the sound of running water. I decided to find out what she was doing.

The bathroom door was slightly ajar, and I quietly got off the couch and tiptoed to the bathroom door. In the medicine cabinet mirror I saw my mother injecting herself with a syringe. At the time, I didn't know about drugs. Shit, I didn't know what they were or what they looked like. All I'd heard about drugs was they were bad for you.

Confused about why my mother was sticking a needle in her arm, I pushed the bathroom door open and tried to find out. "Ma," I asked, "what are you doing?"

Before I could take a step into the bathroom, my mother began to yell and curse at me in a way that took me by surprise. "Boy, get the fuck out of here . . . and close that fucking door!"

Stunned by her Jekyll-and-Hyde change, I froze in the doorway, unable to move. My mother hadn't ever cursed at me, and it made me feel for a split second as if she hated me. I finally closed the door and stumbled back to the couch, where I started crying. I was definitely a momma's boy back then.

I must have cried myself to sleep on the couch because when I woke up, I was lying down with my head on my mother's lap. She was gently rubbing my head, and when she saw I was awake, she gave me a kiss and said she was sorry for yelling and cursing at me. She promised she would never do it again and gave me another kiss, telling me she loved me.

What I didn't know was that my mother was a drug addict. She'd been shooting up with cocaine for eight years. What I also didn't know was that she had been raised by adoptive parents, and she had another son named Corey who was ten years old. She put him up for adoption before I was born.

Several days after I found her shooting up in the bathroom, my mother showed me a picture of a Black boy and told me he was my brother. He resembled me, but his eyes were slanted a little as if he were Asian. I looked more like my mother with the same brown eyes, the same jaw line, and I had her full lips. My brother's lips were bigger.

"Ma, is this my *real* brother?" I asked excitedly as I stared at the small, faded photo she handed me.

"Yeah, that's your *real* brother, boy," she said, grinning.

"Do we have the same fathers, Ma?"

"No. Ya'll got different fathers but ya'll are brothers just the same."

"Where he live at, Ma?"

"He stay in South Carolina with his adoptive parents. Mr. and Mrs. Harrison."

"But why don't he live with us, Ma?"

"Because," my mother said, letting out a deep sigh.

"Because why, Ma?"

"Because I *had* to put him up for adoption."

"Why'd you have to do that?"

"Malcolm, stop asking me all these questions. Go on in the living room and play that Atari or watch the TV or something." She didn't want to talk about my brother.

My mother gave birth to Corey Jamal Jordan on April 10, 1972, inside the Toland Village Detention Center for Girls. When she was seventeen years old, she was in a relationship with a weed dealer she started seeing after Corey's father dumped her when he found out she was pregnant. Her new boyfriend talked her into transporting a pound of marijuana to a house across town, and when she got there, the cops were waiting for her. She got charged with drug trafficking, and in spite of her plea that she was seven months pregnant and a first-time offender, she got a one-year sentence. Two months later, after she gave birth to my brother, a Department of Human Services social worker talked her into signing away her custody rights to an adoption agency. The social worker said it was the best thing for my brother.

A few months after my mother signed away the custody rights, she started having regrets, and then she had a complete change of heart. She decided to try to regain her parental rights and get Corey back. She wrote to the Cuyahoga County Department of Human Services, but she ran into bureaucratic roadblocks. She was released from the juvenile detention center in March of 1973 and went right downtown to the Department of Human Services, where a shift supervisor told her there was no way to undo an adoption. She refused to give up, and for the next two weeks she caught the bus from her Y.M.C.A. room across town to the DHS building, looking for somebody who could help her. She kept trying, but after several failed attempts, she finally gave up. The dark reality that she wasn't going to get Corey back finally hit her, and it left her in a state of deep depression that in a matter of weeks put her in the saddle on that beautiful white horse called *Cocaine*. She came to love *Cocaine* as deeply as if he were her surrogate son. She didn't know that by the time she was done riding her beautiful white horse, it would be a filthy, uncontrollable, bucking beast in a rodeo that was a living hell.

Chapter Three

Toward the end of the summer of 1982, during dinner, my mother told me we were finally about to move out of the projects and into a house.

"Where we moving to, Ma?" I asked, trying to smile with a mouthful of spaghetti.

"We moving out east on Lee Road. Moving in with a friend of mine."

"Who is it, Ma?"

"Somebody I met, boy. . . . Now stop being so nosey, and quit talking with your mouth full."

I swallowed my food, but I didn't stop asking questions. "Is your friend a man or a lady?"

My mother smiled across the table at me, and she stared at me for a while before she answered. "It's a guy named Larry Shelton. Anything else you want to know, Mr. Inquisitive?"

"How old is he?"

"Forty-eight."

"FORTY EIGHT!" I yelled, laughing. "That's thirty years older than you, Ma."

"It's not *thirty* years, silly. It's twenty-one years. Now finish eating so you can take your grown-up self outside or something."

The next week, my mother introduced me to her boyfriend when she invited him over for dinner. I can't remember what we had for dinner. I didn't eat it because I lost my appetite the moment I saw my mother's boyfriend. He was around six four and fat, a dark-skinned, ugly ass nigga whose face looked like a walrus. All I could think was: what in the world did my mother see in this dude. Black is beautiful, but this motherfucker was so fucking black he could leave fingerprints on charcoal. The only reason I could think of for why my mother wanted to be with this dude was *he must have had a bunch of money*. He showed up in an all black four-door Cadillac that looked brand new, but I never asked him if it was or wasn't. As a matter of fact, I never said a word to him that night.

"Ma, can I please be excused?"

"Excused for what?"

"Because . . . ," I said in the low, whining way I talked when I was disappointed.

"Because what, Malcolm?"

"Because I ain't hungry," I replied with a trace of sarcasm.

"You ain't being excused," my mother said sternly. "You go sit here until you done eating."

Not willing to concede, I kept with my case to be excused from dinner. "I'm not eating!"

Before my mother could say anything her ugly ass boyfriend jumped in. "Wait a minute, Angela. . . . Are you go let this boy talk back to you like this? I'm telling you right now, when ya'll move in, he not go be talking back like this staying under my roof."

I looked at my mother to see what her reaction was going to be, and she just looked at me. She said nothing, as if she was saying, "Yeah, right, Malcolm. You ain't go be talking back like that under his roof."

How could my mother take sides against me when I was *her* son? Never in a million years did I think my mother would side against me for anything or anybody, and here it was. She was doing just that with her "feature-creature" boyfriend. I was so mad if somebody had cracked an egg on my head, it would have fried.

After sitting still at the dinner table for a long five minutes, I got up and walked into the living room, not caring what my mother had said. I just wanted to get out of her and Larry's presence. I sat down on the couch and looked out of the corner of my eye, back toward the kitchen, to see if my mother was going to do anything about it, but she just kept talking to Larry as if nothing else in the world mattered except him. I sat in the living room for a while, and then I got up and left the apartment. She didn't even look my way. This was the start of a long journey that would get longer as I tried to fill the void my mother created when she sided with her boyfriend against me.

The next week we moved in with him. Like us, Lawrence "Larry" Shelton stayed on the east side of the city, but he stayed in a real good neighborhood, right on the edge of an upper class suburb. His house, a beige one-story, trimmed in brown, had a two-car garage with a huge driveway and huge yard. Inside, the house had three bedrooms, two bathrooms, a basement outfitted with a bar and recreation room with a pool table. Overall, it was pretty luxurious, and it offered living conditions *way* better than the place where we'd been.

Two weeks went by after we moved in with Larry, and everything was going kind of smoothly considering I still didn't like him. But I was content with the situation. I had my bedroom sanctuary where I could retreat when I didn't want to deal with my mother shunning me for Larry or with him trying to play the father in my life. All I had to do was shut my bedroom door, turn on the TV, and block 'em the hell out.

I started school at Martin Luther King Elementary a couple of weeks late after the summer break because of a procedural mix-up. It was a fifteen-minute walk from our house on Lee Road. I walked Monday through Thursday, but Larry usually drove me on Fridays before he took my mother to work. He had the day off. He was a senior sales manager at a General Motors dealership, and he worked a flexible forty-hour week. Basically, he seemed to work when he wanted to.

I didn't know anybody at my new school, but my move to Martin Luther King went pretty smoothly anyway. I was the "new boy" so I was the center of attention practically wherever I went. My teacher, a White, middle-aged woman named Ms. Washington, was pretty cool. She didn't seem to mind if her students occasionally talked in a low tone, as long as we finished our class assignments.

My class had about 25 students, and everybody in the class was Black. And out of the twenty-five, two-thirds were girls, which made my schooldays that much more enjoyable. I was starting to take a keen interest in girls, and a few of the ones in my class caught my attention. But nobody caught my attention the way Ericka Daniels did. She was the prettiest girl in the school, and every boy seemed to be in awe of her. I wrote her a letter about once a week for a whole semester, but the little heartbreaker wasn't feeling the kid. I did make friends with three of the boys in my class: Clayton Simpson, Donny Jones, and Pernell Edwards. Clayton and Donny were Pernell's friends and I bonded with them through him. Pernell was the class clown, and I took a liking to him from day one. This kid was a straight up comedian who could hold his own with Richard Pryor telling jokes. He was good with the insults too: "Your mother so stupid she got locked in the grocery store and *starved* to death. Your mother so strong she can *blow bubbles* with Now & Laters!"

Me and Pernell wound up being best friends later in the school year. We pledged to be "niggas-for-life" before we ever heard of the legendary rap group NWA.

Chapter Four

Three weeks before my first Christmas with Larry, I was in the kitchen around 9 o'clock at night looking through the refrigerator, trying to decided on what I wanted to take to my room, when out of nowhere I heard a series of loud, rapid screams. I recognized the voice screaming. It was my mother's. I flew down the hall to her bedroom and Larry's. The door was closed, and I grabbed the doorknob with both hands, but the door was locked. I started to panic. My mother was still screaming at the top of her lungs, and I started to fear for her life. With both of my fists I started pounding on the door. "Open the door. Open the door," I yelled.

The screams came to a stop, and I heard Larry say something about "leaving it alone," but I didn't know what the hell he was talking about. After that, my mother unlocked the door and came out. Her lip was busted, and she had a swollen cheek. Larry had walked in on her when she was shooting up, and he jumped on her. I hadn't ever seen her get beat up by anybody, and after seeing her face, I made a vow to myself that if Larry ever put his hand on my mother again, I was going to do my best to put him underground, inside a cemetery.

I talked to my mother the day after Larry beat her up, and I tried to tell her we should move out. But she said we weren't moving, and she said Larry wasn't going to hit her any more. How she could say that with her face still swollen up like a grapefruit was mind-boggling to me. But surprisingly, Larry got his act together after that, and he and my mother didn't have any more physical fights until years later although they still argued.

Christmas was a week away, and I could barely wait because I already knew what presents I had coming to me. I knew there wasn't any Santa Claus who went down people's chimneys, and my mother knew I knew. So instead of contributing to the perpetuation of one of the longest running fibs in the world, she had me tell her what I wanted, and she went out and bought it. This year was no different except my mother told me I had to get all good grades on my report card if I wanted my presents. But I was used to getting good grades so that didn't seem to be a problem.

Ms. Washington passed out report cards for the first semester on the day before Christmas vacation. I scanned mine and saw the usual good grades. But just as I was about to close it, I saw I'd gotten a fucking U (unsatisfactory) for a behavior grade. I couldn't believe it.

"Ms. Washington! Ms. Washington!" I shouted across the room.

"What is it, Malcolm?"

"Can I come up to your desk, please?" I asked.

"Sure," she said. "Just keep your voice down, okay."

I walked to the front of the class. "Why did I get a U on my behavior, Ms. Washington?" I asked. "I haven't gotten in trouble since I came here."

"Malcolm, you're a good student and one of the brightest in our class. But you do way too much goofing off."

"All I do is talk, Ms. Washington, and you said we could talk."

"I did say that, Malcolm. But you and your buddies are loud and disruptive to the rest of the class, and I have to tell you two or three times every day to keep the noise down. It's nothing major, Malcolm, but I just want you to be more attentive in class."

I couldn't believe my teacher had pulled this shit on me, talking about how I'm disruptive in class. Now I was faced with the possibility of my mother pulling the plug on my Christmas.

When my mother got home from work, I greeted her with a hug and kiss. That was my normal routine. But I held the hug longer than usual, and she noticed.

"Boy, you in a good mood today," she said, grinning and raising her eyebrow. "What you than did?"

"I ain't done nothing, Ma."

"Well, I know one thing—you better not have gotten no bad marks on that report card. I thought you was supposed to get it before Christmas vacation. So where is it?"

I should have known the big hug would be a dead giveaway. I handed the card to my mother and watched her closely. She was smiling as she looked it over so maybe she wasn't going to make a big deal of one little bad grade. But just when I thought I was going to be able to slide past her, she flipped the script on me.

"Malcolm, I know this ain't no U I'm looking at on this card," my mother said, holding it inches away from my face. "Tell me this ain't what I think it is."

"Ma, I ain't even do nothing to get that grade," I said.

"You did something, or you wouldn't have gotten it!"

"No, I didn't."

"Well, I told you what was go happen if you got any bad grades. What did I say?"

"That you was go take my Christmas presents back to the store."

She did it. She took them all back, and I didn't get a single gift. I stopped talking to her for at least a month. This was when my behavior started to get rebellious and I started to drift away from her. I started spending more time over at Pernell's house with the rest of the crew. I was hardly ever at home, and I was staying out till midnight on some school days. My mother tried to put her foot down, but I ignored her and kept doing what I wanted. Larry even locked me out of the house a few times, but my mother would let me back in. This led to them arguing in the middle of the night. It would be constant chaos and confusion between them two or three times a week.

One night I heard Larry really put it to her about me. "You not go keep letting that boy run in here, back-and-forth, in-and-out, just doing what the fuck he want to," Larry said. "I pay the bills here, and I'm fed up with the bullshit."

“I put him on punishments, Larry,” she said. “What else you want me to do? If you stop treating him like he in the army, maybe he stop acting he way he act.”

“Don’t no child control me, Angela!” Larry shouted. “I control the child. And I’m telling you, you better get his ass together. I don’t care if I ain’t his father, if he keep coming in here in the middle of the night, I’m go whip his ass.”

“No you ain’t, Larry. You ain’t go lay a hand on my son.”

“Okay then, Angela. If you don’t like what the fuck I say goes inside my house, then you take your little bastard ass child, pack ya’ll shit, and get the fuck out!”

Every time they argued, it ended up with Larry giving my mother an ultimatum. She could conform to his dictatorship or pack her bags and get out. This was one of his tactics to control her. Now I know he’d done it before—he enticed women into relationships by putting their impoverishment face-to-face against his upper middle class lifestyle. My mother, a single parent with a cocaine habit, living in the ghetto, fell right into his trap.

Chapter Five

(The Summer of 1986)

Nearly four years had gone by since my mother and I moved in with Larry. Some kind of way their dysfunctional relationship was standing up to time and the cocaine. It was hard to believe, considering there wasn't a day went by when they weren't arguing over something.

I still spent most of my time over at Pernell's house when I wasn't at school, just to get away from the constant commotion. One night, around 11 o'clock, I had just gotten back from playing video games over at Pernell's, when I came in the house and saw my mother sitting at the dining room table and crying. Her face was bruised, and her eyes were swollen up so bad they resembled overcooked pepperoni on a pizza.

I knew instantly what had happened to her. Larry had beat her up. . . *again.* He hadn't put his hands on her that way since nearly four years ago, after we moved in. But that didn't matter. He was going to have to pay.

I tried to ask my mother what happened, but she held her hand out like a traffic cop and cut me off in mid-sentence. "Don't say anything, Malcolm. I'm okay. . . . I just need some time to be alone right now. You watch TV in your room tonight because he drunk, and I don't want him snapping at you when he come back in here."

I respected her wish and stayed in my room that night, but I didn't watch any TV. My mind was focused on one thing: killing Larry.

As I laid on my bed, I started to formulate my plan of how I was going to kill him. My first thought was to get a knife and sneak up on him and stab him to death, but I gave way that idea for a much easier one that I'd seen in a movie. I was going to throw a plugged-in electric appliance in the tub while he took a bath. His days of beating on my mother were about to be over.

The next day was Saturday, and I woke up early, around 6:30 a.m.. The first thing I did was look out my window to see if Larry's car was in the driveway, and it was. Then I tiptoed to my door and pressed my ear against it so I could tell if my mother and Larry were still asleep. I stood there for about ten minutes, listening for any kind of sound, and I didn't hear a thing. Satisfied that they were still asleep, I eased out of my bedroom door in my underwear and down the stairs to the basement, where I picked up the 50-foot extension cord they kept in the laundry room. I took it upstairs to my room, hid it in the closet, and went down to fix myself a gigantic bowl of Captain Crunch, which I took back to my room. Then I closed and locked the door and ate the most electrifying breakfast of my life while I waited for my electrifying window of opportunity.

Later in the morning my mother knocked on my door and asked if I wanted her to fix me anything for breakfast. I told her I'd already eaten, and she gave me a big hug and told me to clean up my room and give her all my dirty laundry. I gave her my dirty clothes and closed and locked the door again. A surge of adrenaline rushed through me then, and my heart started beating a thousand miles an hour. Larry always took his bath while my mother cooked breakfast, and I knew it would be just a matter of minutes before he got up to take his bath. I was nervous as hell.

Ten minutes later, right on schedule, I could hear Larry running his bath. I got the extension cord out of my closet and quickly unraveled it and plugged it into my wall socket. I unplugged my GE wood-grain clock radio from the same socket and plugged it into the extension cord. I turned the volume all the way down on the radio, switched it on, and set it on the floor in front of my bedroom door. I could hear the water still running in the bathtub so I waited to be sure he'd gotten into the water. While I waited, I unlocked my door and looked up and down the hallway to make sure my mother wasn't anywhere close by. The coast was clear.

After what seemed like an eternity, the water stopped running, and I heard the sound of splashing. I picked up the radio and grabbed the end of extension cord so the radio wouldn't come unplugged, and in five or six quick steps, I was up the hallway and outside the bathroom. The door was cracked open, and with all my strength I busted through the doorway and threw the radio into the soapy bathwater. I caught Larry completely off guard, and he never stood a chance of getting out of harm's way. When the radio hit the water, he let out an ear-piercing, girlish-like scream that sounded like death. His eyes rolled back in his head, and his naked, obese body started convulsing and flopping around like a fish out of water. Just as I began to believe Larry's punk ass was actually about to die right in front of me, I heard a popping sound, and the bathroom light went out.

When the lights went out, my mother yelled out my name, and I could hear her running upstairs. "What was that scream, Malcolm?" she yelled when she got to the top of the stairs. "What's that cord coming out of your room?"

I couldn't move my lips to say anything. When she realized the cord was running into the bathroom, she took off following it, and when she went through the door, she started screaming hysterically.

I sat down in the hall and tried to think, and then I just started crying. My mother was screaming Larry's name, telling him to wake up, and I thought he wasn't going to be waking up. But I thought wrong! I heard a bunch of splashing and then a series of coughs, and I knew Larry was alive.

I got up off the floor in a panic. It hadn't even occurred to me that he could survive. My mother yelled for me to come in the bathroom, but I took off down the hall and ran outside. I had to get out of the house because if Larry continued his miraculous recovery, I was sure he'd try to kill me.

When I got outside, I ran into the field across the street and hid in deep grass. I hadn't been lying there long when an ambulance and two police cars pulled up. The paramedics and policemen jumped out of their vehicles and ran inside. No sooner had they gone in than three officers, all White, middle-aged males, came out of the front door with their guns drawn. They separated and started looking for me in back of the house, in the garage, and inside our neighbors' garages. Then they huddled in the driveway beside our house, and I could tell by the way they were pointing that they were heading over to the field. Seconds later, they came across the street, split up again, and started combing through the grass.

My first instinct was to try to get deeper into the field because I was only about twenty yards from the street. But I realized they would almost surely see me moving so I laid down, completely motionless, stiff as a mummy. One of the officers was right in front of me, maybe twenty feet from me, but unbelievably he didn't see me. I thought I was in the clear, but just as he was about to walk by me, a small flock of birds took flight from the grass, and the officer turned towards them. When he turned, he looked down, right into my eyes.

"Freeze!" he yelled, and he pointed his revolver right at me. He yelled he'd found me, but the other two officers were already running toward me. When they arrived, I was on the ground, on my stomach, with my arms extended above my head. One of the pigs grabbed me by the back of my shirt collar and yanked me off the ground and dragged me across the street to Larry's house.

They led me up the front porch steps into the house, and then it was the same thing all over again. My mother was sitting at the dining room table crying, and when she saw me, she went off.

"Why you do that, Malcolm?" she yelled, and she stamped her feet. "You nearly killed him! And now you got yourself in all kinds of trouble."

"He always be hitting you, Ma!" I shouted back. "And you don't never do nothing about it! Never!" I could see the officers looking at my mother's face, which was still badly swollen and bruised. But they didn't say a word about her injuries. They probably didn't care.

"You can't just kill somebody," she said. "What were you thinking? I didn't raise you to be like that."

I couldn't offer a response. I stood there dumbfounded until one of the officers read me my Miranda rights. I didn't expect her to congratulate me for trying to kill Larry while the police were standing there, but I didn't expect her to chew me out like that either. The person I tried to eradicate had been abusing her for years.

After he read me my rights, the officer told my mother about the various post-arrest scenarios I was facing, and reality started to set in. I was going to jail.

"Ms. Jordan, the paramedics think Mr. Shelton should make a full recovery. They just need to take him to the hospital and run some tests. That's the good news. The bad news is we're probably going to have to place your son in the Detention Home."

"But can't ya'll just release him to my custody?" she asked.

"After we process him at the station, we'll contact the Detention Home and see if *they* want to keep him or release him back to your custody until the hearing. If they tell us they want to keep him, which they've done with nearly all the kids we've arrested, then we'll take him over to University Hospital for a psychiatric evaluation. If they decide your son isn't in his right frame of mind, the hospital will admit him to their Children's Mental Health Ward. That's not likely, but it's a possibility."

My mother began crying again. "I understand, sir," she said. "I understand."

I'd never been in the Detention Home, but I'd heard horrific stories about it, and from what I heard, it was a place where I didn't want to be. So as the officers put me in the backseat of their squad car and I watched my mother break down again, the reality hit me: whether I wanted to be in the

Detention Home or not, I no longer had anything to say about it or about *anything* because I had officially become a criminal.

Chapter Six

The Detention Home, as the officer predicted, decided to keep me. After spending two hours at the police station getting processed, I was taken to the hospital for my psychiatric evaluation. All I could think about on the way was how to get out of the fix I was in. No way did I want to go to the Detention Home, and it looked like the only thing that could keep me out was a shrink's "determination" on whether I was insane.

The only thing I could think to do was shut down when they asked me questions. I wasn't sure this tactic could accomplish anything, but I had to try something to frustrate the evaluation process, or I was going to be on my way to the Detention Home for sure.

The two officers took me to a small room with a desk and three chairs, and they put me in a chair and left out of the room. I sat there for about ten minutes without moving, and then a short, middle-aged man in a white medical jacket came in with a file folder. He looked Middle-Eastern, and he introduced himself with a thick Arabic accent.

"My name is Dr. Ali, and I am a social services psychiatrist. I give mental health evaluations for young people who are recommended for placement in the Detention Home. I'll ask you a few questions, and you should do your best to answer them as well as you can. Okay?"

I understood what the doctor said, but I stuck with my plan. I was totally non-responsive, didn't even blink.

He continued. "In my file it says you allegedly tried to kill your step-father, or is it? . . . no, your mother's boyfriend. It says you threw a plugged-in radio in the bathtub while he was bathing. Is this true, Malcolm?"

I stared at the wall behind him and didn't say a word, pretended he wasn't even in the room.

"You can nod your head if you don't want to speak. But I need you to respond. I need you to answer these questions so I can make sure you're okay."

Dr. Ali kept trying, but I kept my cool and stayed silent. After repeated attempts to get me to say something, he got up and left out of the room. After while he came back with an older White woman he introduced as Dr. Novak. She was his supervisor, he said. He had told her my story, he said, and explained about my silence. Right in front of me, he asked her if she thought I should be admitted to the CMH Ward, and she looked me over and said I should.

When I heard her tell him I should be admitted, I just about lost it I was so happy! I'd already managed to outsmart *two* psychiatrists and avoided getting stuck in the Detention Home. An eleven-year-old kid wasn't supposed to be able to do that. But I must have tapped into some kind of intelligence I didn't know I had. I found a way to sidestep the long arm of the law.

They took me to another floor, where I had to sit in a room with a male nurse for a couple of hours while they processed me. It was after midnight when Dr. Ali and a female nurse came to take me to the CMH Ward, which was on the third floor of an annex. As we walked, Dr. Ali told me the CMH unit staff would meet with me in the morning and tell me about the rules and regulations. He said he had talked with my mother, and she would bring some of my clothes in the morning. He said we were allowed to wear our own clothes on the Ward. I listened to Dr. Ali but still pretended to be disconnected from reality, and I didn't respond to anything he said.

When we arrived at the CMH Ward, somebody buzzed us through a double door, and a heavy-set Black woman introduced herself to me as Frankie. She talked quietly with Dr. Ali for a few minutes, and then she escorted me to my sleeping quarters. When I got to my room there were clean sheets and a blanket neatly folded at the end of my bed, and I probably set a world record for making a bed and falling asleep. I was exhausted. When my head hit the pillow, I was out like a light.

The first things I noticed in the morning were some toiletries on the nightstand by my bed. There was a small bathroom connected with my room, and I used it. Once I got myself together, I ventured out into the Ward to see what was up and to find myself some food.

There was a pretty Asian woman standing down the hallway with a clipboard, and when she saw me, she started toward me.

"Malcolm?" she said quietly with a soft smile. I nodded. "Good morning. My name is Ms. Ming, and I'm a staff therapist here. I'm going to be taking you through orientation, just helping you get to know all the rules and regulations on the Ward. And I'll introduce you to the staff and some of the residents. You should feel free to ask me questions. But first let's get you some breakfast, and maybe you can meet some of the residents who got up for breakfast."

As soon as I walked through the door to the dining hall, I was totally surprised to see boys *and girls* there! Nobody had said I'd be living with females on an everyday basis.

There were only six residents eating breakfast when I walked into the dining hall. Four of them were White males, and the other two were girls. One was White, the second Latina, a very pretty, caramel-complexioned 12-year-old named Kandi Sanchez. I found out she was a native of Cleveland, and she was absolutely beautiful. It didn't take long before she was my under-the-radar girlfriend.

After breakfast, Ms. Ming showed me around the ward although there wasn't really that much to see. The ward was a long hallway with a TV room and a laundry room next to each other on one end of the hall and a kitchen and dining room, also next to each other, at the other end. The twelve bedrooms opened off the hallway, along with two unoccupied, windowless, padded rooms that were used for residents who were out of control or on suicide watch.

The rules and regulations weren't bad. We weren't allowed under any circumstances to be inside another resident's bedroom. We weren't allowed to use profanity. We went to bed at 10:00 p.m. on weekdays and 11:00 p.m. on weekends. We had to attend "self-esteem group" meetings five days a week for two hours a day, which took the place of school. There weren't any classes because of budget cuts. Life on the CMH Ward was uncomplicated. It beat the lock-up.

My mother didn't come to visit until three days after I arrived on the ward. The visiting room was on the first floor of the CMH building, and as soon as I got off the elevator, I saw my mother and sprinted into her open arms.

"Why you wait so long to visit me, Ma?" I asked.

"Larry wouldn't let me use the car like he told me he would," she said. "I had to take a day off from work and catch a cab up here."

I sucked my teeth in disgust. I couldn't believe my mother was *still* putting up with Larry's bullshit. She let him beat on her, and now she was letting him interfere with her seeing me. I changed the subject. "Am I going to jail, Ma?"

"I'm not sure what's going to happen, Malcolm. They charged you with attempted murder, which is very serious. But it's hard for me to imagine them locking you up. You're only eleven years old. . . . I'm going to try to get Larry—some kind of way—to speak on your behalf when you go to court. But right now he won't even let me use the car to come see you so I'm going to have to work on that." She was silent for a while. "But what I want to know, Malcolm, is what you told these people to get them to put you here? You know good-and-well, Malcolm, you ain't crazy."

"I didn't tell them nothing, Ma. I just stayed quiet every time the man asked me something."

"You stayed quiet?" My mother looked confused.

"Yeah, I just sat there and didn't say nothing. . . ."

"So you just pretended to be crazy?"

I didn't want to tell her I'd been deceptive or manipulative. It seemed like something she wouldn't like, but I couldn't keep from grinning.

"Boy, I can't believe you," she said, smiling. "Give your mother a hug, you little con artist."

We talked for the whole two hours we were allowed for the visitation, and when she had to leave, I gave her another hug and a kiss. And I told her I loved her. She had tears in her eyes as she walked out the door, and it occurred to me that she was heading back into a world that was a lot like mine in the hospital. She didn't have much freedom.

Chapter Seven

It was April of 1987, and I'd been in the CMH Ward for nearly eight months. I'd turned twelve in March, but my time in the Ward made me feel a lot older. It seems to me I grew up quickly.

During my eight months on the Ward, I went to court twice, and both times my judge continued the proceedings to a later date. Except for talking with Kandi I kept to myself. The other residents did seem to have serious mental health issues. I had days when I would get depressed, wishing I was back home hanging out, but the other residents talked to themselves, talked to imaginary people, hit their heads on walls, and some of them screamed at the top of their lungs, which I found annoying as hell.

Kandi was the only person who seemed close to normal, but she was suicidal. Before she was admitted, she told me, she'd tried twice to kill herself. Her stepfather had raped her when she was eleven, and when she told her mother about it, her mother didn't call the police. Instead she covered up for the guy. Kandi overdosed on a pain medication, and her mother had to take her to the emergency room. The hospital released her back to her mother's custody, and a week later her little brother, Mario, found her in her bedroom in a pool of blood. She slit her wrists. They took her to the same hospital, but this time they got her to talk with a psychiatrist, a Black woman, and Kandi told her about being raped by her stepfather. The psychiatrist, Dr. Everett, blew the whistle. The stepfather and the mother both ended up getting arrested, and Mario ended up in foster care.

Kandi was still pretty messed up, but she was my ace-boon-coon while I was at the Ward. I loved that girl.

I went to court for the last time at the end of April. My mother and Larry were there, along with my court-appointed attorney, a short Black guy by the name of Thomas Reed. He had told us after my first court hearing that I wasn't going to be committed to the Youth Department of Corrections, but I wasn't optimistic, considering I'd already admitted I was guilty. My judge, an older Black lady, was supposed to be the fairest, most lenient judge in the Cuyahoga County Juvenile Court system. But it was hard to imagine how she could be lenient with me, just give me a slap on the wrist the way my attorney predicted she'd do.

"All rise!" the bailiff ordered as he started the court proceeding. "Ladies and gentlemen, the honorable Judge Gwendolyn Johnson. Court is now in session."

The judge took her bench and everyone sat down. After the judge entered my case in the record with the court stenographer, she got right down to business. "Okay," she said in a surprisingly relaxed tone of voice, "Mr. Malcolm X. Jordan, how are you doing, young man."

"I'm doing okay, your honor," I said, looking her in the eye.

"How are they treating you over at the CMH Ward?" she asked, putting on her glasses.

"They treating me okay," I replied.

"Are they feeding you good?" the judge asked with a smile on her aged face. "It sure looks like you've gained some weight since I saw you last."

"Yeah, they feeding me good, your honor." I smiled and nodded my head.

The judge turned her attention away from me and greeted everybody else almost as if it were an afterthought. Then she looked back at me.

"Do you know why you're here in court today, Malcolm?"

"Yes mam."

"Why are you in court today?"

"Because, umm. . . I'm charged with attempted murder." I spoke with my head down, feeling ashamed to admit I'd tried to kill Larry.

"That's correct, Malcolm. You're here today because you were charged with committing the crime of attempted murder. You made an open admission of guilt to the court in your previous appearance, and due to your admission of guilt, today I am going to administer your sentence. Do you understand all of this, Malcolm? That you *are* being sentenced today?"

"Yes, you honor. I understand," I said. I was beginning to feel nausea, realizing I was probably about to be incarcerated.

"Attempted murder is a very serious charge, Malcolm," Judge Johnson continued, looking down through the glasses that rested on the bridge of her nose. "I don't believe you're a bad child at all, Malcolm. In fact, I think you're a very bright and intelligent young man, and you can grow up to be very successful in life if you put your mind to it. However, I think you have some serious issues with your temper. You have a bad temper for someone your age, and if you don't get some help dealing with your anger, you're going to end up spending your life in a prison cell or, worse, you might end up dead. You don't want this to happen to you, do you?"

"No, mam," I replied.

"Then you're going to have to pull it together, Malcolm. We have enough Black men dead or in jail already, and we don't need any more. . . . Now, I've stayed in contact with the CMH staff, and I've spoken to them every other week about you. In our conversations and in the weekly reports I've read they say you refrained from talking to anybody but your mother when she came to visit. I don't think you're insane, but it's very abnormal for someone your age—or for anyone—to go months at a time without talking to people. I was very concerned for your wellbeing at first, but then the staff noticed you were talking to *someone* other than your mother, someone they said you were *very* fond of. Do you know who I'm talking about, Mr. Jordan."

I shook my head *no* and tried not to smile because I knew the judge was talking about Kandi. But it was pointless to deny it because my face lit up like a sunrise at the thought of her.

The judge continued. "I believe the *someone* goes by the name of Kandi. *Now* do you know who I'm talking about, Mr. Jordan?"

"Yes, Mam," I said, smiling from ear to ear.

"Okay, then. I thought I might have to remind you that you aren't allowed to tell fibs in court. . . . I was worried about you at first, but once I heard that you made a friend, that you were talking to *somebody* on the Ward, I talked with the CMH staff about the possibility of releasing you into a group home. But nearly everybody thought you needed to be in a more isolated, controlled environment. I thought about that for a few weeks, and I've finally decided to accept the recommendations of the CMH staff therapist and Dr. Ali. I'm going to commit you to a residential placement called George Junior Republic, which—"

"Your Honor," my lawyer said loudly, standing and interrupting the judge. "May I approach the bench?"

"Counsel may approach the bench," the judge replied.

As my lawyer made his way toward the judge, I looked over my shoulder at my mother, who was sitting two rows behind me with Larry's punk ass, and I could tell she was nervous. She was slowly rocking back and forth in her seat with her arms folded, and she leaned forward as though she hoped to hear the judge and my lawyer. Before I turned back, my eyes caught Larry's, and he stared like a Pit Bull sizing up a Chihuahua for his next meal. He was still upset that I had tried to get an apprenticeship as an *electrician* at his expense.

I turned around and tried to key in on what the attorney and judge were disagreeing about, but I couldn't tell what they were saying. My lawyer was emphatically twisting his head back and forth in disagreement. Whatever it was, it ended suddenly, when he threw his hand up in surrender. He turned away from the judge and walked back toward me, looking as if he'd just been in the ring with Mike Tyson. That's when I knew I'd be going away.

"Malcolm, the judge says you're going to have to go to the residential placement," he whispered to me as he sat down and put his hand on my shoulder. "This is not what I was hoping for, but I can't be too upset with the judge's ruling because going to a residential placement is way better than going to jail. George Junior Republic isn't that bad of place, Malcolm. It's like a really big group home. The only thing that bothers me is it's out of state."

"Out of state?" I said, practically shouting. "What does that mean?"

He signaled for me to quiet down. "The placement is in Pennsylvania, Malcolm. But you'll only have to be there for a year if you stay out of trouble."

"Ma!" I yelled. I turned and looked at her and started to cry. "They sending me out of state, Ma."

She put her hands over her face, and she was crying too. When I saw that, it was the first time I totally regretted trying to kill Larry. My mother had already been through too much bullshit in her life with losing my brother, and here she was about to lose another son.

After I was committed to George Junior Republic in late April, it was six more months until I was actually sent there in October. All kinds of paperwork had to be filled out and processed before I could be transferred across the state line. The most important was the "consent and waiver" form my mother had to sign, giving up all her custodial rights. She was already familiar with that one, having signed one years earlier when she gave up my brother for adoption.

Chapter Eight

Right after my court hearing I was assigned a social worker from the Department of Human Services named Todd Littlefield. He was a White guy in his late forties, and he told me what he knew about George Junior Republic. He said he'd be driving me there once all the paperwork was processed. A few months later I had a final visit with my mother, and the next day Mr. Littlefield picked me up in his Jeep and drove me to Pennsylvania.

It took a little under two hours for us to get to George Junior Republic, which was located in the middle of western Pennsylvania, and I was shocked by how big the place was. I had imagined a small colony of houses but it was like a college campus. There were more than twenty-five group homes sprawled over the landscape, and in addition to the group homes GJR had two gymnasiums, an Olympic size indoor pool, an outdoor pool, a track and football field, a horse farm, their own school, and more than thirty outdoor basketball courts. They even had a putt-putt golf course! George Junior Republic Drive ran right through the GJR campus, as well as through nearby Grove City.

After arriving at the placement I was taken to a red brick building, the Diagnostic Center, where all new residents went through a sixty-day orientation before being transferred to a group home. As soon as I walked through the door a fat White guy handed me some clothing and a pair of Chuck Taylor high-top gym shoes. This caught me by surprise because my social worker had told my mother and me that we wore all our own clothes. I found out later that was true, but we didn't get to wear them until after we finished orientation. I changed into the red sweats, and as soon as I had them on, I was homesick. Something about being dressed like everybody else made me feel like I was in jail or the Detention Home. It made me feel like I was locked up.

Besides having to wear the red sweats, we had a bunch of rules to follow, and I could tell right away they'd be a pain in the ass. If we wanted to use the bathroom, play a board game, write a letter, or even get a drink of water, we had to get permission from one of the three staff who worked each shift. Besides getting permission for everything, we had to earn daily "privilege points" just to have the *opportunity* to play the board game.

All the residents in the Diagnostic Center were between twelve and fourteen except for one Black kid named Thomas. He was sixteen. Including me, there were twelve residents, and we were all Black. Everybody seemed to be from Pittsburgh except this one cat named Antwone Hill who was from Cleveland, like me.

"What's up, man?" Antwone asked me. "Where you from?"

"Cleveland," I told him, feeling proud and trying to make my voice sound deep.

"Yeah?" he flashed a huge smile on his chubby, brown-skinned face. "That's where I'm from too."

"What street you stayed on?" I asked him.

"93rd and Hough. Where you stayed?"

"I lived on Lee Road before I came here, but I'm really from Morris Black," I said.

"I can't believe I finally got a homeboy in here!" Antwone said.

We became best of friends in no time. We were damn near like Siamese twins. Where you saw him, you saw me. We *had* to stick together because the Pittsburgh dudes hated anybody who wasn't from their city. They particularly hated people from Cleveland. This was due to the NFL rivalry between the Browns and the Steelers, and unfortunately for Antwone and me, it was football season when we were in orientation.

But orientation went pretty well despite the hostile Pittsburgh hyenas. Antwone finished a few weeks before me, and he got transferred to a "Special Needs" group home, and I lucked out and got transferred to the same home when I was done. The only difference between the "Special Needs" homes and others at GJR was that we could be prescribed psychotropic medications. Also, we went to school in our home instead of the main campus school. We had a classroom that doubled as a library.

Just like he did when I arrived at the Diagnostic Center, Antwone gave me the rundown on all the rules and showed me the ropes. They were pretty much the same as in the Diagnostic Center, but here we were allowed to go in each other's room with permission from a staff member. And we had to attend "Rationale Resolve" group therapy three times a week, run by a drill-sergeant of a social worker, Mr. Monroe. But I had no complaints. I just hoped I didn't have to stay at GJR until my eighteenth birthday, which was possible.

There were sixteen residents in the group home, and most of them were Black and from Pittsburgh. We had three White residents. The Pittsburgh residents weren't as rugged and abrasive as the ones I met in the Diagnostic Center. They were more nerdy and passive. I didn't see any of them as a threat, but I should have remembered--you can't judge a book by its cover.

Chapter Nine

I hadn't ever stayed away from home except for the stint at the CMH Ward, which didn't bother me much. I'd seen my mother on a regular basis at CMH, but at GJR I was hundreds of miles from her. Fortunately, I was able to keep my mind off being away from home by playing basketball.

The smaller of the two gyms at GJR had a full-length court, and it was annexed to our home. We played there with three other Special Needs homes. When there wasn't anybody scheduled for the gym, or if one of the other homes cancelled, our staff let us play basketball. When they offered extra recreation time, only a few people from our house usually went to the gym, which gave me a half-court to practice.

Basketball was already my favorite sport before I came to GJR, but I'd never played much in an organized setting. I had some decent skills, too, but I still hadn't learned some fundamentals.

One day I was shooting around just before the New Year's holiday, and one of the recreation staff, a short, Black guy I hadn't seen before, was sitting in the bleachers. After I'd shot and missed an awkward, mid-range jump shot, he yelled, "Flick your wrist when you shoot, youngster."

I paused and looked toward him and nodded my head. When I took my next shot, I flicked my wrist when I released the ball.

"Like that?" I asked, and I stopped to look across the gym at him.

"Yeah!" he shouted, smiling and clapping his hands. "That's it, youngster, just like that."

After I shot a few more jumpers with my new wrist-flicking technique, he came out on the court.

"What's your name, youngster?"

"Malcolm."

"Where you from?"

"Cleveland."

"Oh yeah?" He laughed. "I got some cousins up there. Always asking me to move up there. . . . But, yeah youngster, you look like you got a pretty decent game. How old are you?"

"Twelve," I said.

"Twelve? I thought you were at least fourteen, the way you look out there. You got a real nice looking game, man, for a twelve-year-old. You might can play for us one day."

"Play for *y'all*?" I was puzzled. "We got a team here?"

"Yeah, we got a team here, youngster! You ain't know that?"

"Naw," I said. "Nobody never said nothing about a basketball team."

"We got a varsity team here and a junior varsity," he said, and I began to wish he'd tell me his name. "You're too young to play right now. You got to be in the eighth grade to play junior varsity and the ninth grade to play varsity. And if you only twelve, you probably in what—the sixth or seventh?"

"I'm supposed to be in the seventh right now, but I got to wait till they start me in school."

"Well, when you get to the eighth, if you keep working at it, you'll be ready, young Malcolm."

"Can you help me work on my game?" I asked.

"Yeah, I'll help you when I can. Normally, I don't work down here. They always have me up at the big gym. Plus, we in the middle of basketball season, and we have to travel away to *all* our games so I spend a bunch of time helping everybody get ready for our bus rides. But whenever they have me down here, I can come get you, and we go work! I'm telling you now, youngster, if I work with you, you got to be serious. You got to *work hard.* Nothing in life comes without hard work, without sacrifice. You hear me, youngster?"

"I hear you. . . . What's your name, man?"

"Tim Harrison," he said, and he looked at his watch. "I gotta get up to the big gym. I'm running late, youngster. Meantime, keep working on that jump shot and stay out of trouble."

I took a liking to Tim right away. Meeting him was like finding a big brother I'd always wanted. He came across as a guy who cared about me, and meeting him uplifted my spirits, made me want to be successful at *something.* I'm sure Tim had no idea how powerfully his words of encouragement moved me.

After settling in at the home, I started school in the middle of the school year, in early February. Because I'd missed so much school since being arrested eighteen months earlier, I had to take a bunch of tests to determine what grade I was supposed to start in. I was placed in the seventh grade, which meant I didn't have to go back. My teacher told me I could have started in the eighth grade if I hadn't scored so low on my math test, which surprised me after being out of school for so long.

Back in school, I did okay with a respectable 3.2 gpa on my first report card, and the year seemed to fly by. We had two months until summer vacation, and I was excited because that meant basketball try-outs would be just around the corner.

I practiced whenever I got a chance through the rest of the school year. Plus, I found out I was 5' 9", and last time I'd checked I was only 5' 6". My chances of making the team were good, according to Tim.

When I wasn't playing basketball, I hung out with Antwone. We talked about girls, wondering what the hell it felt like to get some pussy, or just chilling in one of our rooms, listening to RUN-DMC or Public Enemy on his boom box. I stayed out of trouble too, but I did get into a few verbal skirmishes with a couple of residents every once in a while, usually over wanting to watch a TV program. But everything was okay, as far as my *behavior* was concerned.

We got to make one twenty-minute phone call on Saturday nights, and I called my mother. But she was hardly ever at home when I called. Sometimes Larry would answer, and in a snobbish-ass voice he'd tell me she wasn't there, and then the ignorant son-of-a-bitch would hang up on me. One time when I called he yelled in the phone, "The junkie bitch ain't here." And he hung up.

I missed her, but I was starting to get pissed off at her because she *knew* I'd be calling on Saturday, but she was never there to catch my calls. She did write me about once a month, and she sent me $10 or $20 to put on my spending account. But even in her letters she let me down. She told me excuses why she missed my calls and made promises to be at home the next time, but it was always the same thing—she wasn't there.

I kept calling her on Saturday evenings, and finally one Saturday she was there.

"Hello," she said, and I knew her voice.

"Ma!" I said. "You at home!"

"Boy, I told you I was go be here," she replied in a soft voice, sucking her teeth at the end of her sentence. "You gotta have a *little* faith in your mother, don't you?"

"Yeah," I admitted.

"Well okay then. Have some faith in your mother. How you doing in there though? You holding up?"

"Yeah, I'm doing okay, I guess."

"You getting into any trouble?"

"Naw, I ain't getting in no trouble, Ma. I'm just playing basketball, trying—"

"Playing basketball," she interrupted. "When did you start playing basketball."

"I always played, Ma."

"When?" She sounded doubtful. "I never seen you play."

"I played up at the park and sometimes over at Pernell's house." And I realized she hadn't ever noticed that I played because she was probably too busy doing drugs.

"So they got a basketball team there?"

"Yep. That's what I was go tell you. I'm trying out for the team next season. I'm go make the team, and after that I'm going to college. I'm go play for Ohio State or Georgetown and then the NBA, Ma."

"You can do anything you want in life, Malcolm, but you gotta stick with it. And you gotta work hard! You're going through some hard times now, but you gotta keep your chin up. I know you feel sad and miss being back here around your friends, but you gotta stay positive and keep at that basketball. And don't ever think I don't care about you, Malcolm. I'm going through my own problems right now, and I know I haven't been the best mother in the world, but you are my son, and I love you *and* your brother. Are you listening to me?"

"I hear you, Ma. I'm listening."

"But like I said, you gotta stick with that basketball, and at night, before you go to bed, I want you to get down on your knees and pray to God to give you the strength to go through this."

I listened to everything she said, but I let the prayer talk go in one ear and out the other. I wasn't religious, and the thought of saying a prayer before I went to bed seemed strange, like a fairytale.

When I called the next Saturday, my mother answered again, which put a huge smile on my face. And in the middle of our conversation she asked if I'd been praying. I didn't want to disappoint her so I lied and told her I prayed every night.

I didn't have to worry about lying again because after that call I didn't speak to her again for four years. A few days after we talked, she got arrested for stealing an old white woman's purse from inside a department store. The police found her sitting at a bus stop less than an hour after she took the purse, and when they patted her down, they found a checkbook stolen from somebody else. She went to court a few weeks later and wound up getting only three years of probation.

But six days later her luck ran out. She got caught with two grams of cocaine and a syringe, and when she went before the judge for violating the terms of her probation, she was sentenced to 3-to-5 years at the Jemison Correctional Institution for Women.

I found this out from my social worker at GJR a month after she was incarcerated, and it depressed me. It wasn't so much that she was sent to prison but the fact that she didn't write me a single letter to let me know what was up. My sadness began to feel more and more like anger.

The absence of my mother made me frustrated and bitter, and after learning she was in prison, I felt like a walking time bomb.

I tried hard to control my anger when I wasn't playing basketball, but on the court I let it go, trying to turn it into motivation. It must have worked because my basketball game flourished in that bad time.

Chapter Ten

"Good luck, my nigga!"

Those were the last words I heard from Antwone's big-ass mouth as I left out of the Special Needs home and headed over to the main campus gym. It was time for tryouts for the 1988-89 George Junior Republic Tigers junior varsity. I felt like I had a thousand butterflies fighting for rebounds in my stomach as I walked that wet road. Our group home was pretty isolated so I hadn't been able to play against the rest of the guys who'd be trying for a spot on one of the two teams. I was nervous as hell.

As soon as I entered the gym lobby, I could hear a hundred basketballs bouncing. When I got to the gym entrance, I had to stop and take in the action. There were people everywhere! There were coaches with whistles hanging around their necks and at least a hundred residents warming up for the tryouts. Nearly all of them were Black, maybe ten whites and Hispanics altogether. It seemed like two-thirds of the residents were over six feet tall, and I saw at least five that looked to be 6' 6" or better.

All I could think was, "I hope none of those big motherfuckers dunk on me."

It started like we were trying out for a track team. For the first two hours we just ran our asses off. The coaches divided us into ten groups, and each group formed a single file behind the baseline so we could do "suicides." We took turns sprinting as fast as we could to the nearest free-throw line, then back to the baseline, then to the half-court line and back, then to the free-throw line at the other end, then back, and finally to the other baseline and back. I don't know who called it "suicide," but he knew what he was talking about. By the time we were into our fourth rotation, I felt dead. My lungs were on fire, and my legs felt like cooked noodles.

Somehow I managed to stay in the drill, but a bunch of the other guys didn't make it. Nearly a third of the whole group quit during the "suicides." They got kicked out of the gym, one by one. That was my introduction to the head coach, Jerome Flynt, a big dark-skinned man with a goatee. If you quit on him, he said, you had to get the hell out of his gym, and he meant it. Even that first day, I understood that Coach Flynt was trying to build strength and character in his players.

I held on through that first day and didn't get cut, but I didn't feel like celebrating. My body was sore, and I was exhausted. That night I hung out in my room and kicked it with Antwone, listening to the radio and just talking shit like we did everyday. I had to spar with Antwone whenever we talked just to get a word in because he loved to take over any conversation with stuff about his idol, Mike Tyson, or how much he'd like to fuck Whitney Houston or Lisa Bonet. And I didn't mind talking about Lisa Bonet because I lusted over her my own damn self every time I watched the Cosby show. But *every* conversation was entirely too much to be talking about pussy or boxing. On this particular night, surprisingly, Antwone wanted to talk about basketball.

"You think you go make the team?" he asked me, bobbing his head to a RUN-DMC song.

"Yeah, I should make it, Mike Tyson wannabe."

"Aw, man, now why I got to be a Tyson wannabe?"

I was laughing now. "Cause you is!"

"Man," Antwone continued, "if I'm a Tyson, you a Michael Jordan wannabe."

"Nigga, I'm *better* than Michael Jordan."

"Yeah, right." He had a smirk on his face. "Man, Michael Jordan will beat the shit out of you if ya'll played one-on-one. The score a be a million to nothing, nigga."

"It be a million to nothing if he played *you*," I shot back, "cause *you know* you ain't got no game."

After shooting the breeze with Antwone for a few hours, I kicked him out of my room and called it a night. I went to sleep early. The second day of tryouts started at 3:00 p.m.

the next day, but the way my body hurt, I needed all the rest I could get.

When I woke up the next morning my whole body was sore. I took a shower before breakfast and got rid of some of the soreness. I ate a couple of bowls of cereal and went back to my room and listened to the radio with headphones and the volume up as loud as it would go. I listened for three hours straight, and then somebody behind me grabbed my shoulder.

"Whoa!" I yelled, and I jumped out of my chair, turning around to see who had come up on me like that. It was Tim. I took my headphones off. "Man, are you crazy?"

Tim doubled over, holding his stomach and laughing like crazy. "Boy, you about jumped out of your motherfucking skin," he said when he stopped laughing.

"No I didn't," I replied, and I turned the radio off.

"Bullshit! You shaking like a crap game *right now*," he said as he hopped up on my desk to sit. "Just wanted to see if you ready for this big day."

"I'm ready, man," I said, smiling. "I'm ready now for real."

"Well, *you better be* for real." He straightened his Steelers cap, getting serious all of a sudden. "And you better wipe the smirk off your face. They not go be bullshitting up there today. Maybe you did your thing yesterday, but running suicides and lay-up drills ain't nothing compared to what you'll be doing today. You go be scrimmaging, five on five. You go be going up against guys who run faster and jumper higher than you. If you go be make that team, you got to play harder than you ever played. All that stuff we done in the gym ain't go mean nothing if you don't play hard. You hear me?

"Yeah," I said. "I hear you. I'm listening."

"You better be listening. I want you to make that team—if for nothing else, maybe you can stop bugging the hell out of me." Tim smiled.

Before Tim left, he gave me a quick hug and a playful slap upside my head, the way a big brother might wish his kid brother good luck. It was the kind of thing that made me realize he *really did* care about me, unlike most of the staff at GJR, who either yelled and cursed at us or ignored us. Tim was *real*, and I admired him for *always* keeping it real.

There was no way I could let Tim down. I wanted to make him proud of me.

I had to make the team.

"Gentlemen," Coach Flynt began, as he peered out over the remaining GJR Tiger hopefuls, "all of you know why you're here today. You know what's at stake. We got forty players now, and tonight we'll have twenty-four. Sixteen of ya'll are going out the door, and it's up to you. *You* are in control now, not me or anybody else in the gym. If you want to make one of the two teams, you better bust your ass. Play harder than you ever played in your life."

Just as Tim had told me, we began the second day scrimmaging five on five. Coach Flynt divided us into eight teams that were intentionally not matched. He didn't say so, but it was obvious as hell. Four of the teams, including the one I was on, had skinny players no taller than six feet, and the other four had the muscular, taller players.

I knew coaches liked to match a smaller team against a bigger one like that in other sports. This "David versus Goliath" format was supposed to show which players had the heart to compete against bigger opponents like Goliath. And it showed which players had the killer instinct to put away a physically inferior opponent like David.

Each team played the team they were matched up against twice. The recreation staff officiated, and the first team to score ten baskets won. My team lost our first scrimmage 10-2. I scored one of the two points on a fast break, but judging by Coach Flynt's reaction, you would have thought I put it in the wrong basket.

"What the *fuck* was that bullshit out there?" he shouted as he paced back and forth in front of our team, spraying us with small specks of saliva, like Bobby Knight. "I ought to kick every last one of ya out of here right now! Matter of fact, get ya'll asses back out there. Play again, right now, and if ya'll don't score more than two points, it's bye-bye for every one of you."

We began the second scrimmage just the way we did the first, conceding the opening jump ball so we could keep them from getting a quick bucket. We played zone defense the first time, but after they kicked our asses so bad, we decided to take a chance with man-to-man. It worked at first, and we held them scoreless for a while. But they made some adjustments, and their size and athleticism began to pay off. We got within two points of a tie at 6-4, and then it was all over. We lost 10-4.

Before the start of our first scrimmage, I felt pretty sure I could make the team. After playing the second one, I wasn't so sure. I didn't score any points in the second scrimmage, and I didn't get any rebounds, and when we walked off the court, nobody gave anybody on my team a clap on the back for doing better. Bad sign! But the only thing I could do was sit down and wait until the end of the tryouts. My fate was sealed.

Coach Flynt delivered the "moment of truth" an hour after the second scrimmage. "Listen up, gentlemen," he began. He held up a sheet of paper. "We do this real simple. If I read your name off, congratulations. You just made the team if you're academically eligible. If I don't read your name off, well, better luck next year. So here we go: Steve Vire. . . Tyrone Vire. . . Steve Cooper. . . Jerry Smiley. . . Ricky Dews. . . Melvin King. . . Alton Brown. . . Clyde Scott. . . Carlos Sanders. . . Elvis Currenton. . . Robert Mahone. . . Shawn Carter. . . William Owens. . . Keenan Williams. . . Royce Martin. . . Latrell Mangum. . . Kendrick Worthy. . . Chris Turner. . . Raheem Atwater. . . Mason Simms. . . Tommy Evans. . . Antonio Fields. . . Omar Livingston. . . and last but not least, Tashawn Bryant."

As soon as I heard the last of the names he called, I damn near exploded! I'd already admitted to myself that I might not make the team, but after I heard Antonio Fields and Jerry Smiley's name, I thought *for sure* I'd make it. Both of them were bums. Neither of them could outplay *me on my worst day*! To hear Coach Flynt tell it though, they had.

Fuck!

Chapter Eleven

"Get off me, you fat bitch," I shouted at the top of my lungs. I was trying to free myself from the holds of two white male Special Needs staffers. They had me on the floor inside a yellow, fully padded timeout room in the group home. "Get off me! I ain't do nothing!"

"You calm down, we go let you up," one of the sweaty pigs said as he put his knee on my right arm. "All you got to do is follow directions, keep the damn noise down, and none of this happens."

"Man," I yelled, "I can't feel my arm, can't feel my legs."

"If we get off, you go calm down?"

"Yeah."

"Okay. We go let you up. But you do anything stupid, you going down on the floor face first, *and* we go get the nurse down here again to shoot your ass up."

It was the third time in a week that they'd restrained me, and the other times they shot me with Thorazine to calm me down. It was almost a year since I'd gotten cut from the basketball team, and the restraining seemed almost routine.

I'd been getting in all kinds of trouble. I started arguments with the staff and with residents, and a couple times I started fights for no reason at all except I was miserable. I couldn't get my behavior under control, which made me feel contempt for myself, as well as everybody else. Maybe the worst day, as I look back now, was when I started a fight in the dining room with a kid from Pittsburgh, Ike, and got Antwone kicked out of the group home. It started with an argument about nothing, but Ike took the bait, and I sucker-punched him and busted his nose. He was dazed, and I followed up with a combination, planning to knock him out before he got a chance to come back at me.

While I was doing my Muhammad Ali impersonation, one of Ike's Pittsburgh friends came up behind me and cracked me in the head with a vacuum cleaner. He just about knocked *me* out, and I went down, bleeding from a gash.

Antwone was maybe thirty feet away when I started the fight, and he had a hard time seeing what was happening. But once he seen me get hit in the head, he came after the dude with the vacuum cleaner and sucker-punched *him.* The kid dropped the vacuum and took off, and Antwone picked up the vacuum and went after him.

The kid was fast, and Antwone couldn't catch him. But in the midst of all the confusion one of the residents flipped the dinner table over and started yelling, "Kill 'em all, kill 'em all." Then the whole place erupted into bedlam with guys throwing everything that wasn't bolted to the floor. Staff came running from all over campus, and I got put on a stretcher and rushed to the infirmary. They cleaned me up and put eighteen stitches in my head, and I was back in the group home four hours later.

Antwone was already gone when I got back. When I asked staff where he was and what happened to the stuff in his room, they told me the supervisor decided the two of us couldn't be in the same living area. We were a "riot risk," he said, and they moved Antwone to a group home on the other side of campus. They told me he just about had to be physically removed when they told him. He didn't want to be separated from me. It was understandable. Being from Cleveland, it was in our DNA to stick together, and I fucked it up.

In addition to getting Antwone kicked out of the group home, my fight with Ike also ended my once-upon-a-time, big brother/little brother relationship with Tim. After I got cut from the basketball team, Tim reminded me about it every time he got a chance. "That's why you ain't make the team," he'd say whenever I screwed up. He started on me one day over a careless move I made while we were playing checkers, and I teed off on his nagging ass.

"*Pay attention* to the board, man," Tim said as he was collecting the checkers after triple-jumping me. "That's why you ain't make the team."

"Fuck you, man," I shot back, scowling big time. "Why you always got to say something about *that*? Maybe that's why your son a retard and got cerebral palsy."

Tim stiffened and looked hard at me. We'd talked about his three year old son's handicap, but I never said anything like that before. Tim stood up with fist clenched, and he banged one on the table. "What the fuck you just say? I *know* you ain't just make fun of my son."

"Yep," I smirked, knowing I'd just gotten under his skin. "That's what I said."

Tim spoke quietly through gritted teeth. "I been treating you like my own family, and you turn around and disrespect my son? Don't ever say another word to me, about nothing, the rest of the time you in here. I mean that shit."

Right then I didn't give a fuck if I ever spoke to Tim again the rest of my life. But a few days later I started to regret what I said about his son. Like he said, he had treated me like family. Mad or not, I should never have disrespected his son or him. I was dead wrong.

After falling out with Tim I didn't see him for a couple of months. When I did, I tried to apologize, but he wouldn't even acknowledge that I was there. I'd hoped he'd let bygones be bygones, but he stayed true to his word.

After falling out with Tim, I just seemed to lose control completely. It was 1989, and in addition to starting arguments and fights I started breaking windows and throwing chairs, and I flipped a school desk over.

My social worker, Mr. Monroe, set up a "behavioral intervention conference" with the resident staff, and they tried to figure a way to do something besides restrain me and shoot me up with Thorazine. They decided to put me on a special "behavior plan." They said my behavior was disrupting the whole group home, and I needed to be *isolated.* What they meant by a "behavior plan" was really solitary confinement.

I had to get up every day at 6:30 a.m. and go to the conference room in the back of the group home, and I had to stay in the room *all day*, seven days a week, until 8:00 p.m. The only thing I could have in the room was schoolwork, which I refused to do, and some library books, which I never read because they were westerns and science fiction, which I hated. There was a table and chair in the room, and a couch, where I spent most of my time sleeping or thinking about why I was born. When I wasn't sleeping or pondering the mess that was my life, I played imaginary basketball, putting myself in the NCAA Championship or the NBA Finals. Mostly, my days were a yawning gulf of boredom.

My social worker said I'd have to be on the behavior plan indefinitely, until I showed I could follow the rules and my attitude improved. I figured I'd be there about two weeks, maybe a month, but after two months went by, I started to come unraveled.

Getting stuck in the conference room when I wasn't doing anything defiant except not doing my schoolwork began to feel like torture. I knew I'd caused a bunch of problems, but I didn't think I deserved to be warehoused like a cardboard box.

Four months went by, and I was still on the behavior plan. It was December of 1989, and it was freezing cold in the conference room. The heat was down in the whole group home, and the staff refused to let me take my blankets in the conference room. I stayed in the room for maybe an hour, as long as I could stand it, but finally I said, "fuck everything," and I walked down the hall into the day room and sat down and started watching TV. The staff looked at me like I was crazy. They told me to get back to the conference room, and I ignored them. So they restrained me and put me in the padded room. When they let me out a few hours later, I did the same thing, and they restrained me. This time they called the infirmary and had the nurse come over and shoot me up with some "slow juice." I don't know what it was, but it knocked me out *instantly*! Whatever it was, I didn't want anything else to do with it.

After they shot me up with the mystery drug, I chilled out, and a couple of weeks later they took me off the behavior plan. For a few months everything was cool. Then they moved in some residents from Pittsburgh, and all hell broke loose. I got into two fights in three days—fights I didn't start. And I ended up back on the behavior plan. Pretty soon I was back in the old routine of getting restrained and sedated. I was acting a damn fool.

Chapter Twelve

(One Year Later)

"I need you to come in my office, Malcolm," my social worker, Mr. Monroe, said as he walked past the conference room.

I followed him into his office. "What's up, Mr. Monroe?" I asked, standing in front of his messy desk.

"Have a seat. I got some good news to tell you. I'm pretty sure you're going to like it."

"Good news?" I was suspicious, but I couldn't help getting excited.

"I spoke with your caseworker in Cleveland this morning about your future here at GJR. He wanted to know if you were still on the behavior plan, and I said you were. I said you've been on it off-and-on for two years. He asked if I thought we could help you here, and I had to say honestly I don't think we can. Come this fall you'll be with us four years. You won't go to school. You won't follow the rules. There's just nothing else we can offer you here, Malcolm. Your caseworker agreed with me. We need to try something new."

"So, sounds like ya'll kicking me out."

"We're not kicking you out. We're *discharging* you, and soon, if the paperwork goes through."

"Discharging me where?" I asked. I was getting nervous.

"Back to Cleveland, an independent living program." He looked me in the eye, probably wanting me to know he was being straight with me. "It's a program called 'the Empowerment' that prepares you to live on your own. From what I've heard, it's set up so you start off in a group home for a few months and then move into a low-cost apartment on your own that's paid for by the Empowerment program until you can find a job and take over the rent yourself. They give you some money every week for living expenses up until you turn eighteen."

"Why only up to eighteen?" I asked.

Mr. Monroe chuckled. "Because after you turn eighteen you're on your own! . . . It's a real good program, Malcolm, and I honestly believe you'll be able to do a better job there than you have here."

I hadn't thought much about living on my own, and the idea was intimidating. I didn't even know what my Social Security number was. Living on my own seemed like a major step, but I was ready for anything that felt like change.

"Can I go with you, Ms. Gray?" I asked the thirty-two year old, petite, brown-skinned, *super sexy*, assistant director of my new home, the Empowerment.

"I ain't going nowhere but right down the street to the food bank real quick to pick up some milk and loaves of bread," she replied, looking at me with a devilish grin. "Why you always want to go somewhere with me anyways?"

She knew why I wanted to go with her everywhere. After I arrived at the Empowerment in November of 1991, it took a little more than a month before we began sneaking around. Whenever she had to drive somewhere, she started taking me with her. Sometimes we'd go to a cheap hotel for a half hour and fuck each other's brains out. If we went somewhere close like the food bank, we'd have sex in the Empowerment van or, sometimes, her Chevy Blazer. We only used the Blazer at night though.

I was a virgin when I met Ms. Gray, and after being with males all the time at GJR, getting close to her sent my hormones into overdrive. She was in charge of orientation at the Empowerment so when I first arrived, she was *always* around me. She helped me get enrolled in GED classes, and in the evenings she helped me study for my pre-GED test. She helped me fill out a job application and open a savings account. Basically, she showed me everything that had to do with living on my own. I was grateful, but my main feeling when she came near me was lust.

While I was being tortured by Ms. Gray's sensuality and thinking about her when I wasn't with her, I didn't know she was thinking about me too. She kept her feelings in check during the first several weeks I was at the Empowerment, and I didn't have a clue. Then we went out to lunch after New Years, and I got a very pleasant surprise.

We were talking about why I ended up at GJR, and out of nowhere, Ms. Gray asked, "So tell me, Mr. Malcolm, do you have a girlfriend?"

"Girlfriend?" I was shocked. She sounded almost angry, as if there might be something wrong with me having a girl friend. "Naw, I don't got no girl friend."

"What! You mean to tell me a *handsome* guy like you ain't got now girlfriend?"

"Nope," I smiled. "I ain't got one."

Ms. Gray ran her hand through her long, silky black hair. "Well, I know one thing. If you were little bit older, or I was a little bit younger, I'd let you be my boyfriend as long as you wanted to be."

"Whatever you say," I said, still smiling, wondering again what it would feel like to kiss her sexy, full lips. I shifted my attention from her lips to her eyes, and just as I did, I felt her shoeless foot gently rubbing my dick and upper abdomen. "Damn," I gasped, and I looked around the nearly empty restaurant to see if anyone was looking.

Ms. Gray laughed. She seemed to get a kick out of seeing me react to what she was doing with her foot. "You like that, Malcolm?" Her voice was soft as she continued to massage my member, which was now fully erect.

"Yeah," I said, and I must have sounded a little breathless. Ms. Gray seemed to be trying to make me come, but she sensed what was about to happen, and she stopped in time to spare me from sure embarrassment.

I can't remember if we finished eating, but Ms. Gray took me to a random motel on the west side of the city, and she gave me my first piece of pussy like it was my birthday present. The first time we did it, I came pretty fast, but then we did it again more slowly. I thought I was tired, but she said she wanted to teach me some Latin, and she used those beautiful lips and her tongue in a way that made me shout with pleasure.

Then she stood in front of me naked, in no rush to get dressed. "Did you enjoy yourself, baby?"

"That's the most I *ever* enjoyed *anything*!" I said, rubbing my chin and relishing the moment. I thought I'd crossed a threshold from adolescence into manhood, and I couldn't stop smiling.

"Hmmm, I know that's right," Ms. Gray said, grinning, and then she snapped her fingers. "If you can keep *our* business between us, maybe we can make this a regular thing."

"Well, it's go be regular then because I ain't saying nothing to nobody!" I promised.

Even though Ms. Gray and I continued to get together when we could, at the Empowerment we were careful. There were too many other staff and residents around for us to take chances.

The Empowerment operated a lot like the Special Needs group home at GJR. We had weekly group meetings, and we had a privilege level system too. The staff were permitted to restrain us, but I never saw it happen. There were ten residents including me inside the cramped quarters that had been a regular two-family duplex. *All* of the residents were Black, which was almost true at GJR. Unlike GJR, we were allowed to sign out and go places on our own once we made our privilege levels.

I made my level early in 1992, three months after arriving at the Empowerment. I'd been looking forward to being able to go somewhere on my own so a week before I made my level, I asked Ms. Gray to get me some information about the RTA buses. And the first day I was cleared to sign out, I caught the bus on a freezing cold day and rode across town to my old neighborhood. I was headed for Pernell's house.

My neighborhood had changed a lot. There were businesses where there used to be vacant fields, and there seemed to be action on every corner I rode by.

It took a while to walk to Pernell's house from the bus stop. All the upgrading I saw on the way over hadn't changed anything in Pernell's neighborhood. His house still looked raggedy as hell. I walked to the side door and rang the doorbell, and pretty soon a familiar, muffled voice came through the door. "Who is it?"

"It's Malcolm," I practically shouted. "Is Pernell here?"

"Malcolm? Malcolm who?"

This time I did yell. "Malcolm Jordan."

Before I could say anything else, the door came flying open, and the face I'd connected with that voice appeared. It was Pernell alright. "Malcolm!" he hollered exuberantly. He looked pretty surprised, but he grabbed me and put me in a bear hug. "Man! . . . Where the *fuck* you been at, nigga?"

"They had me in a place called George Junior Republic, in Pennsylvania," I said.

"I heard stories about that place! But come on in, nigga! Let me close this door before my mama kick my ass for letting the heat out."

I couldn't believe how much Pernell had changed. I remembered a skinny kid with a baby face, and you could still see that kid, but he was over 200 pounds, and he had a beard. I was just *starting* to get some peach-fuzz.

"I can't believe how big you got," I said after we got down to his basement, where we hadn't hung out together since 1986.

"You should see that nigga Donny," he said. "He fat as fuck now."

"He still stay on Brigg?" I asked.

"His mother do. He moved with his father over on Union a couple of years ago."

"What's up with Clayton? Where he at?"

Pernell frowned. "He still stay on Lipton, but I don't fuck with that lame no more."

"Why you say that?"

"Man, that nigga got caught with a couple of dime bags of weed, and his snitching ass told the police I gave it to him."

"Man, you bullshitting!" I said.

"I wish. Just got off probation last year because of that bullshit. I gave that rat the weed, and after he told on me, the police came up to the school with a K-9 and found five bags in my locker. They gave me two years of probation for that shit."

When Pernell said he'd gotten caught with some marijuana, it didn't cross my mind to ask if he'd been selling or just smoking it. But when it came time to head back to the Empowerment, I realized he was probably dealing.

"Dig, my nigga," I said. "I got an 8 o'clock curfew." I grabbed my coat and hat. "I got to get going. Got to catch my bus."

"Catch your bus?" Pernell said, sucking his teeth. "Man, what you gotta catch a bus for?"

"Shit, man, so I can get back to the spot."

Pernell smiled and put both of his hands up to his mouth. "Aw, man, I forgot to tell you, didn't I?"

"Tell me what?"

"Nigga, I got an '89 S-10 out there in the garage," Pernell said, with a smirk. "You ain't gotta catch no damn bus, man."

We went out to the garage, and as soon as he pulled up the door--just seeing the *rear* of his truck—I guessed he was dealing. His truck was custom painted dark burgundy with metallic gold flakes in the paint. It had an aerodynamic ground-effects spoiler-kit, an Alpine 1000-watt six speaker CD sound system, chromed-out door panels, and it had tinted windows and chrome rims that protruded out the sides of the wheel wells. I know it's stereotyping and racial profiling to guess Pernell was selling drugs because he had this flossed-out truck. But I wasn't David Duke on the outside looking in, thinking all

Blacks are criminals either. I was *from* the hood, not somebody who *wore* a hood, and I knew what was happening.

"Goddamn, Pernell! What's the story on those rims?"

"Hundred-spoke Daytons," he laughed. "You ain't hip to D's, my nigga?"

"You gotta remember. I been gone for a minute, man. How much those cost?"

"Twelve hundred."

"Twelve hundred!" I said and let out a whistle. "Man, where you get that kind of money?"

Pernell smiled. "I work for the *city*, brother." He unlocked he passenger door. "I'm just like the mayor, my man."

On the way back to the Empowerment Pernell drove me through my old neighborhood. He had some old-school D-Nice in the Alpine, and every time he turned down a side street with people outside, they stopped whatever they were doing and stared into the truck, trying to see who we were as we bobbed our heads to the music. For somebody who didn't get much attention, with the exception of what Ms. Gray gave me, it was a good-ass feeling. It was an endorphin-releasing, natural high, and it made me feel like I was a *movie star*.

The allure of that celebrity feeling that came with riding through the hood in Pernell's truck was powerful. Afterwards, when I got back to the Empowerment, it left me wanting that feeling again even more than I wanted to have sex with Ms. Gray. I guess that should have made me suspicious of myself.

"Stay cool in there, my nigga," Pernell said as I got out of the truck after we exchanged phone numbers.

"Most definitely." As I walked up to the entrance of the Empowerment, I looked at the piece of paper Pernell gave me and saw his number was the same as it was before I got arrested. It made me shake my head and think back on the times we had growing up.

Chapter Thirteen

I was in the Empowerment kitchen when one of the residents yelled from across the living room, "Malcolm!"

"Yeah!"

"The phone's for you."

I walked into the living room and picked up the phone.

"Heyyyy, baby!" It was a cheerful, *recognizable* female voice.

I knew who it was instantly, but I pretended to be confused. "Who is this?"

"Boy," she said, "you mean to tell me you don't know the voice of your own mother?"

"Hey, Ma!" I shouted. "I was just playing with you, Ma. I know your voice anywhere."

"You *better* know it, as long as I had to stay in labor bringing your behind into the world."

"Ma, when you get out?" I asked.

"I was supposed to get out March first, before your birthday, but they screwed up the paperwork and let me out yesterday, on *April Fool's Day*."

We both laughed. "April Fool's Day! That's crazy, Ma. . . .Where you at now?"

She sucked her teeth. "They got me down here in this dirty halfway house on Woodland, across the street from Hot Sauce Williams. It was either come here or go back to Larry's place, and I know you or me wouldn't go for that. I got to stay here a couple weeks before I can leave out on my own or I'd get up there to see you. You can come down here if you can find a way. We get visits on Mondays, Wednesdays, and Fridays from ten in the morning until eight at night. So if you can do it, try to get down here and see your mother, okay?

"I'm go come down there this Friday, Ma. If I have to walk, I'll be there!"

I called Pernell, and he said he'd take me down to see my mother on Friday, which was two days away.

He picked me up after he got out of school, and he drove me down to her halfway house. He waited in his truck for me, which was damned nice of him because my mother and I talked for over four hours, until visiting hours were over.

It was pretty emotional. We hugged for the first time in over four years, and tears ran down both of our faces. All of the resentment I'd felt just vanished. It became an insignificant thing of the past.

I think I held her hand the whole time I was there. She was as beautiful as she'd ever been, but she'd put on a little weight during her time inside. I tried to tell her everything I could remember in my life in the years since we stopped communicating.

"So," she said, as I knew she would, "you been playing basketball?"

"Naw," I admitted, looking down at the cracked floor tiles in the visiting room. "I don't play no more, Ma."

"I thought you wanted to make it to the NBA."

"I did until they cut me from the team," I admitted.

"Cut you from the team? Why'd you get cut from the team? Did you do something wrong?" Her disbelief somehow made me feel better.

"I got cut during tryouts. . . . I guess I wasn't good enough."

She looked me straight in the eye, and it reminded me of when I was little. "Well, you can't give up on something just because it didn't go your way, Malcolm. You're not supposed to quit at *anything*. I didn't raise you to be no quitter. . . . It's going to be plenty of things that's hard through your life, but *you can't quit*. Like that song I used to play when you were little: *You gotta keep on trucking*. It's like the situation with me and your brother Corey. Even though he's grown now, I'm still go do my best to try and make him a part of our lives. I know I wasn't in his life, and I messed up being a mother to him, so far. But that don't mean I'm go just give up on trying to be a mother to him. . . . Don't give up on your dreams, Malcolm. I want you to get back out there on the basketball court so I can see you on TV one day."

I could tell she was giving me some good advice, and it inspired me to give basketball another try. It wasn't so much the "never quit, never give up" stuff that won me over. I'd heard that before. But what got to me was feeling again that she really loved me. She wasn't just going through the motions.

It took a while to get back on the court, but three months after my first visit to her at the halfway house I took the plunge and started playing again at the newly built Emmett Till Recreation Center in my old neighborhood. It wasn't easy after almost four years away from the game. My skills had deteriorated, and my conditioning was terrible. But slowly my game began to resurrect itself.

After two months of hard work on the court, I began to dunk on some big guys, and my defense came back. Accolades were coming my way, and Pernell told me the word on the street was I might be the best in the city.

I didn't let it go to my head the way I had at GJR. But I did come to realize *I really was good*, and I started to entertain the idea of playing in college one day.

Chapter Fourteen

If I wanted to play basketball in college, I was going to have to earn my GED. I took the test, but I didn't study enough, and I failed it by *one point*! I was spending too much time chasing around the very hot Ms. Gray, and I took my eyes off the prize, my education. I was too locked in for much too long on her beautiful, Nubian ass.

Ms. Gray helped me rededicate myself to studying for my second GED test. She started spending all her idle time with one of the new staff at the Empowerment. She kicked me to the curb. It fucked with my head at first, but I was hardly around her anyway, once I started playing ball again. The attraction I once had toward her, so strong I got an erection any time I thought of her, dwindled to nothing.

Everything was going good in my life, as well as my mother's. She'd gotten herself a nice apartment on the west side, plus her after-care program hooked her up with a decent job at a nursing home. I went over to her apartment a couple times a week, and every time I did, she tried to give me ten or twenty dollars. I never accepted because I wanted her to get on her feet all the way. I still didn't have a job, but I got a weekly stipend of $75, plus Pernell looked out for me once in a while with a C-note. So I was straight. Well, everything was going good for about six months, until the January day in 1993 when I found a syringe in my mother's medicine cabinet.

"Why do you got to use this stuff?" I held the syringe in front of her face.

"Use *what*?" She looked at what I held in my hand. "What are you talking about?"

"Don't act stupid, like you don't know what I'm talking about, Ma. It was inside the medicine cabinet."

"What you going through my medicine cabinet for anyways? You supposed to be in there—"

I cut her off. "I thought you wasn't go do no more drugs, Ma! It's just like before. You always promising something, and then you *never* do it."

"Malcolm, you calm down for a second," she said, as she nonchalantly tried to grab the syringe out of my hand.

I jerked my hand back. "No! I'm not calming down about *nothing*!"

"*Who* you raising your voice at, Malcolm?" she shouted back. "I don't give a damn how mad you think you are. You ever raise your voice to me like that again, I'm go knock you into next year, some-fucking-where! And give me that needle."

A month earlier my mother had been fired for getting into an argument with her boss about always being late for work. After she got fired, I started going over to her apartment every other day to give her some moral support, plus I'd finally gotten a job at a bullshit video store, and I gave her half my paycheck every week. She'd told me she was go have to get on welfare and move back to the projects if she didn't find a job. I didn't want that to happen by no means, whatsoever.

I told Pernell about my mother's financial situation, and he gave her enough money for two months' rent. A week later she was insisting she still had to move, and this made me think she was using drugs again. When I found the syringe in her medicine cabinet, my suspicion was confirmed. My mother was strung out *again*.

Chapter Fifteen

When I found out my mother was shooting up again, I left out of her apartment mad as hell and caught the bus across town to Pernell's place.

It was past ten o'clock when I hit Pernell's, and he was surprised to see me. I'd never showed up at his house at night before.

"Man, you lucky I'm home. What's up?" He led me downstairs.

I shook my head. "My mother shooting that shit up again," I said, sitting down on a milk crate.

"Man, you bullshitting?"

"I'm serious. I found a fucking needle in her medicine cabinet, and I knew something was up. We gave her that money, and she still kept telling me she was go have to move."

"She spent all that money on dope?"

"I don't know if she spent it all, plus I ain't seen no dope," I admitted. "But it don't take no rocket scientist to figure the shit out when she got needles in her medicine cabinet and no fucking job."

While I was talking, Pernell pulled a joint and a lighter out of his pants pocket and held them. "You're right," he said, and he tossed me the joint and the lighter.

It caught me by surprise. "What you giving me this for?"

"Fire that bitch up," Pernell said, smirking.

"You know I don't mess with that shit."

"Nigga, quit being scared and *blaze that shit*. It'll take all the bullshit off your mind."

"Man, I ain't scared of nothing," I said, inspecting the joint as I thought about lighting it up. "Don't be trying that reverse psychology on me either, nigga."

I put the joint in my mouth, fired it up, took two deep hits, and held it in as long as I could. It didn't make me choke the way I thought it would. I passed the joint to Pernell and wondered what effect it was go have on me. It took a few minutes after filling my lungs a few times with cannabis, and then the high snuck up on me. “Oh, my God!” I said out loud, and I looked at Pernell with my mouth wide open. It was almost as good a feeling as the first time I had Ms. Gray.

Pernell burst out laughing. “Oh, you like that shit now, huh?”

“Hell yeah, man! . . . I been missing out.”

“I had that same reaction the first time, too. But check this out—I’m go tell you what you *really* been missing.” Pernell looked serious.

“What’s that?” I asked.

“This *free* money, that’s what.”

“What you talking about?”

Pernell continued, still serious. “I’m talking about this dope game, my nigga. You all out here on your own, man, and *you ain’t got no money in your pockets*. I know you got that little job at the video store, but you and I both know that ain’t nothing. And you already said they gonna cut you loose when you turn eighteen. That’s right around the corner. What you go do then?”

I shrugged. “I don’t know, man.”

Pernell continued. “You got to look out for *yourself.* Ain’t *nobody* go look out for you but you!”

“You right on that,” I admitted. “But you know I’m trying to do the college thing, man. I just got my GED last month, and I ain’t planning to fuck that up.”

“I feel you on that, all the way. But the way this shit set up, you not go fuck *nothing* up.” Pernell pulled a wad of money out of his pocket. “You see this right here? This *two grand*, my nigga. I made this in *two days*. You could be making the same thing and *still* go to college.”

“It sound good, but I ain’t never sold no drugs before,” I said. I was thinking about being able to make two thousand dollars in two days.

"Check this out," Pernell said, and he looked down at his watch. "I'm about to drive you back to the spot before you get in trouble for missing your curfew. But tomorrow I'm go swoop you up in the morning before you go to work, and I'm go give you the *whole* rundown on how to get this money."

He picked me up the next day bright and early, and we went back over to his house and smoked some weed, talking about the pros and cons of selling weed.

It started with me against getting involved in the drug trade, but the more Pernell kept talking, the more I got intrigued. We talked about prices, weights, and profits one second, and the next we were talking about how to detect an undercover police officer. I don't know how Pernell did it, but by the time he took me to work, he'd talked me into getting in "the game."

Chapter Sixteen

"How much you make yesterday?" Pernell asked with a smirk.

"Man, stay out of my *business*!" I replied before I let out a small laugh. "What you always trying to count my ends for, anyways?"

"I'm just trying to get you to spend some of that loot with ya, boy." Pernell laughed and opened a pint of chocolate milk.

"I might be to holla at you later on if I get this other half sold. As a matter of fact," I looked at my watch, "let's get out of here."

It was August of 1993, and Pernell and me were on our way out of the apartment I'd gotten six months earlier through the Empowerment, right before I turned eighteen so we could get started with our regular routine of "getting our serve on." I'd been selling marijuana for almost seven months now, and everything Pernell had hyped the experience to be turned out to be just what he said: easy, safe, and *very* lucrative! I had a couple of close calls with the police, and I had to hit a few backyard fences to get away, plus me and Pernell had to issue a little street justice to a few customers that tried to get over on me, but "the game" had treated me real nice.

I started off selling dimebags, and made around $300 to $500 a day right away. After a couple of months of being in the game, though, dimebags began to fade because "blunts," weed-laced cigars just took off. They took ten times more weed to fill one than what it took to roll a joint in an E-Z-Wider rolling paper. When blunts took off, people started buying weed in quarter-ounces, half-ounces, and whole ounces, and dimebags got to be a thing of the past. With the increase in demand my profits soared. I graduated to selling ounces, and Pernell went to selling *whatever you want*.

With the money I was raking in I bought my mother and me thousands of dollars worth of clothes and jewelry. I furnished my apartment and paid the rent for my apartment and my mother's. My biggest buy was my prized possession, a Nissan Maxima, which I got from an Arab storeowner for $6,000 *cash.*

I was ballin' out of control, or at least I thought I was.

In addition to my financial prosperity, I was making it with every woman I wanted. I was shining *hard,* and everywhere I went I had dames all over me, *like syrup on pancakes.* I was living reckless though, hopping from one hotel room to the next, having unprotected one-night stands like AIDS wasn't a fact.

Pernell's relatives had a mini-family reunion on the 4th of July, and he took me with him. He introduced me to his cousin Sharon, and that put a hold on my sleeping around. We started going together two weeks later. She was 5 feet 9, light skinned with green eyes, and the girl was so sexy I would have drunk her dirty bath water if she asked me. Sharon caught me with my nose wide open, and she put it on me, thick like molasses. I fell in lust and love with her in no time.

I enjoyed that summer of 1993 like no other in my life. I enjoyed it too much. Riding around and smoking weed all day put me out of shape, and I smoked my way right off the basketball court. I neglected all the priorities I was supposed to be taking care of to go to college. I'd been meaning to already be enrolled at Cleveland State before the summer was over, but I never even got around to applying for financial aid. I was too caught up in the splendor of the streetlife.

But the summer itself went by smoothly except for the college thing. Pernell's summer didn't go so well. Towards the end of July somebody broke into his house and stole several pounds of weed and over $60,000. He didn't tell me about the break-in for almost two months. There were rumors around the hood that he took a hit, but I didn't think much about them at first because he didn't say anything. Those rumors hung on though. People were saying he'd gotten jacked by way of a "B and E," and I finally asked him if it was true. He said it was true except he wasn't broke like everybody was saying.

So that's why you wanted me to keep re-upping so fast, I thought to myself. After Pernell came clean, I suspected he wasn't as financially solid as he claimed to be. A week later, though, he put an end to that speculation when he showed up on the block in a '91 emerald green Sedan de Ville, sitting on gold, 100-spoke *Daytons*.

"What you want to do, man?" Pernell asked. We were in the Sedan de Ville, waiting for a light. "You want me to drop you off at Sharon's? Or you want to just roll with me and get your blaze on?"

"I'm lightweight tired, man. But I'll ride with you." I adjusted my seat so I could almost lie down.

It was maybe 9:00 p.m. when we started riding around and getting our smoke on, which had gotten to be almost a regular routine ever since I'd gotten into an accident a few weeks earlier. My car was in the shop so I rode around with Pernell. We were riding through the east side, listening to Scarface on *The World is Yours*, and before the CD finished, I dozed off. When I woke up, it was past 1 o'clock, and we were somewhere on the west side, which surprised me because it was the White side of the city, where we *never* kicked it. I asked Pernell why he was driving around on the west side, and he said he'd been over to some White girl's house, somebody he met at Tower City Mall a few weeks earlier. He said they smoked some weed in the backseat while I was sleeping. Knowing him, I guessed they'd done a lot more than smoke back there.

Next thing I knew, I woke up around 3:00 p.m., drowsy as hell, still dressed. I was in my apartment, but couldn't remember being dropped off by Pernell. I was so drowsy and disoriented that I started to call Sharon just to have her come over and sleep in with me. But instead I got up, took a shower, changed clothes, ate some leftover pizza, and paged Pernell. I asked him to come over and swoop me up so I could sell my last three ounces of weed before re-upping.

He had to do a couple of errands for his mother so he didn't get over to my apartment until some time after 7:30 that evening. When he pulled up, I grabbed my Browns pullover jacket, ran out and jumped in his car. I lived on Hulda Avenue, a small side street off East 110th Street, maybe twenty minutes from the block where we sold our drugs on Miles Road. No sooner than I pulled my jacket over my head and we turned onto East 110th, a black-and-white police cruiser was behind us. I didn't panic, and Pernell seemed calm, but we did make it our business to give the tailgating cruiser our full attention. We knew it took only a little slip up to break some law and let them get the drop on us.

"Shit," Pernell said in a whisper-like voice, just sort of talking to himself as he stopped for a traffic light.

Before I could ask him why he said it, I saw reflections of the cruiser's red and blue flashing lights. But I wondered why we were being stopped. When I saw Pernell put the car in "park," my stomach started to churn like a washing machine on the spin cycle. I figured I had a ten second window to jump out of the car and run with my three ounces of weed, but before I could make up my mind to take a chance on getting shot by a trigger-happy cop, a White male officer with an angry, twitching face was glaring down at me through the passenger side window with his gray steel 9mm pistol aimed at my head. A second officer, also a White male, had his gun leveled at Pernell. I froze.

"Driver," the officer next to Pernell said, "I want you to *slowly* turn the car off. Keep your hands where I can see them. . . . Are we clear?"

"Yes—yes, sir," Pernell stammered. He sounded like a runaway slave who'd just been recaptured.

"I didn't know what was happening, but I knew *something* was definitely wrong. The officer on Pernell's side took him out of the car—off the rip—and put him in cuffs. He walked him back to the cruiser and put him in the backseat. Then the officer on my side took me out of the car and patted me down.

"Well, well, well, look what we got here," he said quietly, and he held up the rubber-band-wrapped, zip-loc bag of weed he'd taken out of the pocket of my jacket. "Looks like somebody's going to need a *bunch* of bail money."

He cuffed me and pushed me in the backseat of the cruiser with Pernell. Then he and his partner got in the front and typed something on the computer. A few minutes later both officers got out and started searching Pernell's car.

I didn't waste any time before asking Pernell what was happening. "Nigga, what the fuck you do?"

Pernell sucked his teeth. "I ain't did nothing. . . . What the fuck you tripping on?"

"I ain't tripping, man. Why they cuff you up so quick like that?"

"That's some routine, precautionary shit. . . . Stop being so damned paranoid."

"Yeah, you was sounding nervous as hell, maybe *paranoid*, when they took you out the car."

"Relax, man. I ain't done nothing. And that weed they found on you don't even—"

Just as I was beginning to think he might be right, the cop on *my* side of Pernell's car leaned back and stood up holding a black handgun in the air.

"Motherfucker!" I said, scowling. "Why you ain't tell me you had a gun in the fucking car?"

He just looked at me and shrugged his shoulders. I took a deep breath and shook my head in disgust. When I looked again at Pernell's car the cop *on my side* was holding up a baggie of what I was pretty certain was crack cocaine.

"Naw, man!" I looked at Pernell, not even trying to hide my rage. "You said you ain't sell nothing but weed. Why they keep pulling that shit out from *my side of the car*?"

Pernell had never acted like a coward since I'd known him, but in the back seat of that cruiser he turned into a straight-up bitch. He wouldn't look at me, let alone answer.

After the police finished searching Pernell's car, they came back and asked us about the gun and the baggie. They asked us who owned the gun and the dope, and neither of us said a word. Pernell should have stepped up to the plate and took out. He knew he was dead wrong for not telling me he had a gun and dope stashed in his car, *on my side*.

When we got to the police station, Pernell's coward ass snapped back to reality, and he reconnected with his gift of gab. They started to put us together in a holding cell, but he sensed I might need some physical altercation, and he told the police he didn't want to be around me if we weren't cuffed. They put him in a separate cell, around the corner from where I was, and I never seen Pernell again.

I stayed in that pissy holding area for every bit of six hours before anybody spoke a word to me about anything. Sometime around midnight an older White guy came and fingerprinted me and booked me into the jail. After a while he took me down a hallway and up some stairs to a room with five White guys sitting behind a long table. As he was leading me to my chair, one of the men, a short, fat, balding guy in his late forties, stood up and said, "So heeeere's our stick-up kid."

Stick-up kid? What the hell? The paperweight in front of him said "Detective Thurman." I asked him what he was talking about.

"Have a seat, Mr. Malcolm Jordan." I sat down, and he continued. "You don't ask the questions. We do. But you're wondering why I called you a stick-up kid? You rather be called a stick-up *man*?"

"For what? I ain't robbed nobody."

"Come on now, Mr. Jordan. Don't play fucking stupid. You know what you and your fat-ass friend did over on the west side the other day."

"What we do? We ain't done nothing. What you talking about?"

"Enough with the bullshit. You know what you did. The fucking *gas stations* y'all held up."

"I stood up. "What gas stations?" I yelled. "I ain't robbed no gas stations."

"You did, Mr. Jordan. And sit your ass down and lower your voice in my house."

"Fuck you and your house, man! I ain't robbed nothing or nobody."

"Hey, Mike," the detective yelled across the room to the uniformed officer who fingerprinted me and walked me up there. "Take this fake dope, wax selling, robbing little bitch back to the tank before I fucking lose it."

"Fake dope? What you talking about?" I lowered my voice, trying to get him to explain what he was talking about.

"You know damned well what I'm talking about. But we're not playing this game anymore. You had your chance to talk."

Up until the detective made the comment about *fake dope* and *wax*, I was walking in the dark. But as the officer led me back to the holding area, he told me the shit they found underneath my seat wasn't cocaine. It was *wax* and *flour*. And when he told me this, a light went on. Everything started to crystallize.

Pernell had gotten robbed a couple months earlier. Now I found out he'd been driving around with counterfeit controlled substance, stuff he'd been trying to sell to somebody. He must have been broke all along, just like everybody was saying. More than likely to make it *appear* as if he still had money, he probably got somebody to put his car in their name so he could make monthly payments on it and still convince people he'd outright bought the Sedan de Ville. Plus, he had a gun in the car that he never mentioned to me. It made me think Pernell probably did rob the gas stations some kind of way. If he did, he must have done it while I was asleep in the car on the west side. He'd told me he was in the back seat smoking weed with a White girl, but I ain't *never* known him to kick it with a White girl. None of this dawned on me at the time, but it was making sense now.

The police accused me of robbing gas stations, but I was pretty sure they were trying some elementary tactics to break me down so I'd tell them something about the robberies. But even if I knew he'd robbed the gas stations, I wouldn't have told them a thing. I wasn't going to snitch on anybody. Even if I was a snitch, I didn't have any information. I was asleep when the alleged robberies were going down.

Chapter Seventeen

"It is what it is, young blood." An old-school inmate in a holding cell told me that while I was waiting for my arraignment in the city jail. I was trying to figure out how I could be charged with "aggravated robbery" if I didn't actually participate in the robbery. The old-school cat told me the same thing everybody else did: being "complicit" to an aggravated robbery was the same thing as being a "principal offender," according to the Ohio Revised Code. That meant a person was go face the same time, regardless whether they committed the crime or just orchestrated it from a distance.

When I first got arrested, I was nearly certain the detective that interrogated me was trying to run a game on me. I thought if I stayed strong for a few days, most of the charges—three counts of aggravated robbery, one of drug trafficking, one of carrying a concealed weapon, and one of possession of a counterfeit controlled substance—would be dropped. I figured I'd be released since all I had been caught with, technically, was three ounces of weed.

I figured wrong.

Three days after my arrest, while I was still being held at the district jail, Detective Thurman came to my cell door and told me he'd decided *I orchestrated and ordered Pernell to rob three gas stations.* I don't know where he came up with that bullshit theory, but the next day I was transferred downtown to the city jail and formally charged. I was assigned a court-appointed public defender, and I was given a bond of $164,000 for all my charges. That meant if I wanted to get out of jail, I had to raise ten percent of the $164,000 to give to a bondsman to bail me out. I wasn't optimistic, considering all I had to my name was a couple of thousand dollars stashed in my apartment. I had my car too, but I couldn't get more than a few thousand for it.

After my arraignment I got to use a telephone, and I called my mother. When I told her what I'd been arrested for, she went hysterical. "Malcolm," she shouted when she got herself under control, "you told me you were go stop selling that shit so you could play basketball! You promised me! And here it is, all this time you been out there running in the damned streets. Now look at you. . . . But what they do with the other guy?"

"I don't know what they did with that lame, Ma. I ain't seen him since we got arrested. But look, Ma, I need you to call Sharon for me real quick on the three-way."

"Alright, hold on." My mother clicked over to dial Sharon's number, and I considered how to tell Sharon I had some money stashed at my apartment without letting my mother know. I loved my mother, but if she got wind of some money stashed somewhere while she was still getting high, I'd never see it again.

She clicked back over. "You still there, baby?"

"Yeah, I'm here."

"Alright, there she go. I'm go sit the phone down so ya'll can have some privacy." I heard her sit the phone down, but I knew, nine chances out of ten, she was still on the line.

"Sharon?"

"Boy, what you than did?"

"I ain't done nothing. You need to be asking your punk-ass cousin *what he did.*"

"I already talked to him, and he say they claim ya'll robbed some gas stations."

"Sharon, I don't got time to speak on this shit. The phone go off any minute now. Plus, I ain't about to talk about *nothing* over this hot phone line. But check this out. . . . I need you to go over to my apartment tonight and stay there until I call you sometime tomorrow. I'm supposed to get transferred upstairs to the county jail in the morning. So *make sure* you there to catch my call. I got something important to talk to you about—"

Luckily, I got to tell her that much before the phone clicked off on me. Everything was what it was, though. Once she caught my call, I'd be able to have her retrieve my stash and put it on my books.

The next day at dawn I was transferred upstairs to the sixth floor of the county jail inside the Justice Center, which consisted of two jails plus more than twenty courtrooms in a twenty-two story mini-skyscraper. I was a little nervous because I'd never been in the county jail before, and I'd heard it wasn't no cakewalk.

After breakfast I got to use a phone, and I called my apartment. I let it ring more than twenty times, but nobody answered. So I hung up and called Sharon's mother's house, where she lived, and her mother told me she hadn't seen Sharon since the previous evening. Even though I told Sharon to make sure she didn't miss my call, she did. And I was pissed.

I kept calling my apartment every time I got a chance, but the phone just rang and rang. The next day I called around, trying to track Sharon down. No luck. Nobody knew where she was, and then I called my place again and got a busy signal. *Somebody* was over there, using my phone, and it had to be Sharon. When I redialed, it was still busy, and every time I called back, it was still busy. Against my better judgment I called my mother.

I told her about the stashed money and Sharon, and she said she was going right over there to see what was going on. She told me to call her back in the morning. Then she'd tell me what she found out.

I called her first thing in the morning. She told me that when she knocked on the door of my apartment, she heard loud reggae music playing. Nobody came to the door so she banged nonstop for ten minutes. But nobody came. When she told me this, I felt a surge of anger and adrenaline. When she left, my mother said, she saw something she hadn't noticed on the way in—Pernell's truck parked across the street.

Some kind of way he'd managed to get his snake-in-the-grass ass out of jail, and he'd slithered right into my apartment, probably with his cousin Sharon, who had a spare key. It didn't take me long to put the pieces together. Pernell was the only person I knew who listened to reggae.

I'll probably never know exactly what transpired inside of my apartment. But I know for a fact I've never seen a single dime of the money I stashed there. Sharon pulled a David Copperfield disappearing act on me, and I never saw the fake bitch again. Whatever chance I had at raising some money for making bail was gone.

Chapter Eighteen

Two months after I was arraigned, I met with an attorney for the first time. It was November.

He was young, and he had red hair. "I'm Ronald Harrington," he began, as he stuck out his hand. "I've been appointed by the court to represent you." He sat down and went on, "There are six cases pending against you, and I've only been able to give them a quick scan because I'm up to my fanny in work. What I need to do now is ask you some questions and get more familiar with the facts. Okay with you?"

I nodded. "I'm with you."

"Okay, let's get started then, Mr. Jordan. Or would you rather that I call you Malcolm?

"Whatever you're comfortable with is cool with me."

"Okay, let's make it Malcolm." He took some papers out of a brown accordion file folder and thumbed through them. "It says here you were indicted for three separate aggravated robberies by way of complicity, and there's a concealed weapon charge and two drug offenses. Is that correct?"

"That's right."

"Did you do these things?"

"The only thing I'm guilty of is having weed on me. All the other stuff, I don't know nothing about any of it. I swear!"

"Don't take this the wrong way, Malcolm, but if you did any of the other offenses, I need to know. If I'm going to represent you effectively, I need to know the facts. Otherwise I'm going get surprised in court, and then you're screwed."

"I hear what you're saying. I didn't do anything except have the weed on me. The detective at the district said I *ordered* my co-defendant to rob some fucking gas stations, but that's bullshit."

"What about the gun and the counterfeit drugs? The police report says they found it all under your seat. Did you know about it?"

"Hell no! I would never have been in that car if I knew about the gun and the dummies under my seat."

"Dummies?"

"The fake drugs."

"I see. Well, you probably don't have to worry too much about that charge. It's mainly the robberies. You can bet your co-defendant is going to take the stand against you if you go to trial. Given the little I've seen of the record so far, I think they've got a weak case against you. But you can never tell, especially with all the hungry-for-conviction prosecutors they've got trying cases nowadays. But I need to read this stuff, and I'll get on it next week. Maybe I can have some news for you the next time we get together. I'm thinking you'll have your first pre-trial next month, before Christmas, or maybe early January. So I'll get back in to visit you in two weeks."

Meeting my attorney wasn't encouraging. He was already talking about going to trial, and he hadn't even read my cases. I wanted to kick myself in the ass for not having a *paid* attorney. I should have taken the first few thousand dollars I made selling weed and invested in an attorney. Better yet, I should have stayed the hell away from the unpredictable life of dealing drugs.

Red-headed Ronald Harrington came back in two weeks, as he said he would, but he didn't have any good news. He went through a pile of redundant bullshit that he'd covered in our first meeting before he told me there were five witnesses who made statements that they'd seen me slumped down in the passenger side of the "getaway" car. Then he brought up the stuff from back in the day when I'd tried to kill my mother's abusive boyfriend, Larry. He told me to be ready for a bunch of questions about that because the prosecutor would probably try to paint me as cunning, sophisticated criminal capable of masterminding the robberies. He seemed to be saying the prosecutor would try to make me look like John Gotti or Bumpy Johnson. I couldn't believe it, and I just tried to keep my chin up and stay optimistic.

Chapter Nineteen

"How you doing?" my attorney asked me as I sat down in the nearly empty, damned near freezing courtroom for my *second* pre-trial.

"Okay, I guess. Hoping for something good to happen today."

My first pre-trial, two weeks earlier, right before Christmas, was nothing like what I expected. I thought I'd get to see my judge, the Honorable Donald Marino, an Italian conservative in his early 60's with a reputation for handing out long sentences. But I didn't see him or the prosecutor. I sat in the courtroom with the bailiff the whole time, minus the presence, as usual, of my missing-in-action mother. My attorney hung out in the judge's chambers with the prosecutor, accomplishing nothing, as far as I could tell. After I sat there in limbo for two hours, he had the audacity to come and tell me the prosecutor, Twila Swarhout, was offering me a plea-bargain of *five-to-25-fucking-years.* Swarhout was a White, obese ultra-feminist with an ax to grind against men, and I told my attorney the prosecutor could take the so-called deal and stick it up her fat ass.

My second pre-trial started out the same as the first one. My mother was a no-show, and my attorney, the judge, and the prosecutor spent the first hour in the judge's chambers. My attorney spoke with me briefly before he went in, saying he was going to try to get the aggravated robbery charges dropped. It was hard to imagine that, considering I'd already been presented with a so-called deal of five-to-25 years *for something I didn't do.*

When my attorney finally came out of the judge's chambers, he walked around a wood partition and headed right toward me. I was sitting in the front of the spacious courtroom, cuffed and bellychained in my bright orange jail attire. I watched him approach, trying to read his body language and get a clue about how the conference went. I couldn't read him, but when he sat down, he took a deep breath and exhaled a chest full of air. His breathing unsettled me. Seven years earlier, in my juvenile hearings, my attorney started breathing the same way just before he told me I was headed for GJR. When a lawyer sighs and lets out long deep breaths, bad news is on the way.

"It ain't good, is it?"

He looked kind of embarrassed. "Well. . . . If you were counting on getting the robbery charges thrown out, then things aren't so good. I tried like hell to get those robbery charges off you, Malcolm, but the prosecutor won't budge. She's dead-set on convicting you. But she put a new deal on the table. And for starters the prosecution has developed a stronger case against you since your last pre-trial."

"Stronger how?"

"You know your co-defendant is going to take the stand against you if you go to trial, right?" I nodded. "Well, the prosecutor says your co-defendant is going to testify basically that you ordered him to rob all those gas stations so he could earn his stripes the way you did back in the day when you electrocuted your mother's boyfriend."

I couldn't believe it. "That's total bullshit," I blurted out. "Earn his stripes!"

"Easy, Malcolm. You need a clear head now. This is a serious situation."

"Just tell me what the deal is."

"Right. . . .They're offering you four-to-15 years.

"Four-to-15? How the hell is that a deal?"

"Truth is, Malcolm, you could possibly be out of prison in, say, two-and-a-half years on this deal. Eight months and 15 days counts as a year. On a sentence of four-to-15, you'd go in front of the Parole Board in 34 months. And since you're a first-time offender, if you stay out of trouble, chances are you'll be paroled your first time up."

"I can't do no 34 months for something I ain't do."

"Listen, Malcolm, this is a tough ordeal for you. But if you go to trial and they find you guilty, there's a good chance you won't get out of prison until you're well into your forties."

"My forties? How the hell you figure that?"

Harrington looked like he wanted to be somewhere else. "You go to trial," he said quietly, "and you drag the court through a long, drawn out proceeding, that judge is going to hit you with a harsh sentence. He'll run all your sentences consecutively, and more than likely he'll give you close to the maximum on each charge. You take the deal and you eliminate any chance of this scenario ever happening. Think about it. . . .You could be back on the street in under three years, and you'd still be young when you got out."

I told myself after the first pre-trial if the bogus charges weren't thrown out, I'd box the jury up and go to trial no matter what. But Harrington got to me with his doom and gloom, and I began to consider the reality of being incarcerated until I was in my forties *for something I didn't do*. The thought shook me to the core, and I decided there was no way I could take a chance on going to trial. For once my attorney seemed to know what he was talking about: if I got found guilty, I was going to be locked up for a long-ass-time.

So a couple of hours after the start of my second pre-trial I put an end to the chance of getting sentenced to a marathon term: I pled guilty on all the charges. I signed a plea-agreement, and in exchange for my plea of guilty a week later I was sentenced to an indefinite term of four-to-15 years.

Two weeks later, just a couple days before I was transferred to prison, my mother visited me. We had a good heart-to-heart although I got upset briefly when she said she'd sold my car without consulting me, as she'd agreed to do. She got $1,000 although I'd been pretty sure I could have got $2,500. But I didn't get too bent out of shape because she said she wanted to make sure I had some money on my account to take with me. Plus, she seemed pretty distraught that I was actually headed for prison. She put $500 of the $1,000 on my account.

But I couldn't shake the thought that I was going to prison *for something I didn't do.*

At the end of the visit, when my mother walked out of the visiting room, I had to fight back tears, but I didn't want to embarrass myself in front of all the inmates in that room. That night, back in my bed when everybody was sleeping, I covered my head with my pillow, and I let go.

Chapter Twenty

Two days after the visit, around five in the morning, the third-shift guard woke me up. They called him Old Man Baker, and he shouted at me: "It's moving day, young fella." And I knew the moment I'd been dreading had arrived.

Old Man Baker gave me ten minutes to take care of my hygiene, get dressed, and gather my belongings. Then he took me to a holding cell in the basement, where somebody handed me a bagged breakfast. After I finished eating, I was strip-searched, given an orange jumpsuit, handcuffed and shackled, and led to a black prison transport van. Ten minutes later we were on the Interstate, headed to one of the many modern day slave plantations scattered across the state of Ohio.

Silence engulfed the occupants of the prison transport van as it traveled up the long driveway towards its destination, the Logan Correctional Facility in Woodhill, Ohio, a rural town with a population of 2,200 in northeastern Ohio, forty-five minutes away from the city of Cleveland.

Seven or eight inmates, including me, were being transferred to the LCF prison from the Cuyahoga County Jail, but I paid them hardly any attention. It was winter, early February 1994, and it was freezing inside the transport van. All I could think about was the cold and prison. The combination of cold and nerves, not knowing what to expect of prison life, had me paralyzed.

I'm over six feet, and I weighed about 180 pounds then, none of it fat, so I wasn't afraid so much of being targeted by a bully. Being Black also helped to calm my nerves a little because the way I heard it, it was the White boys who got extorted and sized up to be somebody's subservient penitentiary housewife. *They* were the "fresh meat" the macho penitentiary homosexuals drooled over, the ones who would hear, "shit on my dick or bleed on my knife." It was the White boys who would take a stripping, not me. But all that reasoning didn't help much. I was nervous as hell.

I was an 18-year-old first offender, convicted of "complicity to commit robbery" on multiple counts along with two "drug-related offenses" and a charge of "carrying a concealed weapon" -- and was sentenced to four-to-15 years. On top of that I didn't have any family outside of my mother, and she was a drug addict. I'd never even seen a picture of my father. Going to prison felt like being pushed out of an airplane into the Amazon River with nothing to grab onto.

"Baldheaded hoes! What you see 'D'? Wha-wha-wha 'cha see? I see some baldheaded hoes!" LCF inmates were posted at their cell windows, shouting at us as we were escorted across the yard from Receiving and Delivering to our assigned housing. It didn't make me feel welcome. In addition to the mandatory clean-shaven haircut they were yelling about, we had our blue prison uniforms and our identification numbers. The vulgar shouts, which were actually rap lyrics by Willie D, I learned later, were part of the hazing ritual. The misogynistic rap song was made to ridicule women with short, Grace Jones-like hairstyles. But the shouting LCF inmates hijacked the song and turned it into a raw, in-your-face welcoming song for the baldheaded inmates arriving in the "belly of the beast."

It sounded like a million men were calling me a "baldheaded hoe," and I knew I had to reciprocate in the way of the street. "Tell your mothers to suck my dick," I shouted back at them, figuring they were testing us. Some of the inmates walking with me also returned the verbal disrespect, but some of them were wide-eyed and quiet, unwisely letting it go on without an answer. They were the sitting ducks, and I knew they'd most likely end up on their knees sucking dick or bent over getting fucked in the ass.

It probably took no more than ten minutes to walk to H-Block from Receiving and Delivering. But it seemed like hours. LCF was enormous. It was so big the "yarddog" officers who patrolled the interior of the prison grounds drive golf cart style ATVs on their routine patrols.

I followed four inmates up an ice-covered walkway that led to the entrance of my new home. Once inside, I saw, maybe 200 feet in front of me, two Black inmates almost as young as I was running around a bunk bed and laughing hysterically. They seemed to be playing an adolescent game of "chase," which seemed *bizarre as hell* to me inside a cellblock. Instead of feeling I'd arrived in a hardcore, gladiator-style prison environment, I felt like I'd walked onto the set of a fucking Jerry Springer show.

As soon as we were all inside the cellblock, a middle-aged correctional officer stepped in front of us with a clipboard. He was Black, and he looked very tough. "Listen up, newjacks," he said, barely loud enough for me to hear. "My name is officer Allen, and along with that gentleman sitting over at the desk, Officer Meeks, we'll be your regular first-shift officers Monday through Friday. Like I tell every newjack who comes here, me and Officer Meeks aren't here to fuck with you or make your life miserable. We're easy to get along with. Follow the rules and give us respect, we'll do the same with you. We're here to do our eight hours and make sure you don't kill each other or kill us or kill yourselves. . . . Okay, listen up. If the last digit of your ID number is even, zero or 2 or 4 or 6 or 8, you're moving into a cell. If it's odd, you'll be sleeping on the floor behind me, in the dayroom area."

After sleeping on the floor in the County Jail, I wasn't up for sleeping on the floor of no prison with a million motherfuckers running around like track stars while I tried to sleep. Fortunately for me, my prison ID number, 031-3752, ended with an even number, and I got to move into a cell. I still had to contend with the reality of coexisting with a cellblock full of wild-ass inmates, but that was mainly when we went to the chow hall. At night I didn't have to deal with anybody but my cellmate.

Shortly after Officer Allen finished his welcome speech, Officer Meeks escorted me to my cell. It was on the second tier range of the overcrowded cellblock, which housed 240 inmates even though it was obviously built for less than half that many. "You go be sleeping on the top, Mr. Jordan," the overweight, Al Roker look-alike said as he fumbled with his keys. "You got a good celly, right here. He'll give you the grapes on how things run in here."

I waited for Meeks to open the door. As soon as he swung it open, I heard my cellmate's raspy voice. "You mean to tell me I'm getting another celly *already*?"

Officer Meeks smiled. "Yeah, old knucklehead boy," he shot back. "Now you get on up and help this young brother get situated."

I caught a glimpse of my cellmate as he rolled out of bed with a tee-shirt tied around his head like a doo-rag. He was a young, chubby Black dude. He kind of resembled the rapper Too $hort.

I stepped in and put my property on top of the bed. There was an eerie silence in the cell, but my cellmate finally broke it. "What's your name, man?" I was looking out the window at the snow-covered yard, unable to believe I was really *in prison.*

I looked away from the window. "Malcolm," I said, "Malcolm Jordan."

"Well, my name's Rob, man," he said, and he stuck out his hand. "Where you from?"

"Cleveland," I said, and I leaned over to his bunk, where he was sitting, and I shook his hand.

His face lit up. "Yeah? That's where I'm from too. I stayed on Buckeye."

"Hell, naw. I used to stay a few streets over from there back in the day, when I lived in Morris Black. I moved out on Lee Road, though, in '82 or '83."

"Man, Morris Black is my *stomping grounds*!" Rob said, excitedly. I used to be all up through there everyday with my uncle."

"What's your uncle's name," I asked, and I *was* curious.

"Donald Ray Williams."

"Wait a minute. He the one who owns that boxing gym and carwash on Woodland?"

"Yep, that's my uncle."

"Damn, I ain't know that. . . . I never met your uncle, but I than heard his name a bunch of times over the years."

He stood up and got a cup of water and changed the subject. "What kind of case they got on you, fam?"

I took a deep breath and let it out slowly. "Man, they got me on some fake robbery bullshit. Plus, I got a petty dope case too. They gave me four-to-15 for everything, but my attorney told me I should get out at my first parole hearing."

"What they say you robbed?"

"Fucking gas stations! . . . They put me on some John-Gotti-Al-Capone bullshit, talking about how I *ordered* my co-defendant to rob the stations *while I sat my ass in the getaway car*."

My cellmate, Rob, let out a chuckle. "You serious, man?"

"Hell yeah, I'm serious. My fake-ass co-defendant did all that shit while I was passed out in the car, and then he put it down on me and said *I made him do it*. . . . I don't even know how much time he got."

"Damn, man, you got yourself one crazy case."

I shook my head in disgust. Rob caught on fast. I started making up my bed, and I changed the subject. "So, man, what's up with this place? Give me the rundown."

"Aw, this shit ain't nothing for real, fam. The police don't bother you in here, and damn near all the niggas in here are a bunch of cornballs. You see 'em running around, playing chase and shit when you came in?"

I smiled for the first time in a while. "Hell yeah, I seen that shit. I was, like, what the fuck? And that bald-headed hoe song when we came across the yard, that was crazy!"

Rob laughed. "I felt like killing them bitches, yelling that shit when I came in."

"So how long we have to stay here, and how long we stuck in this cell every day?"

"No telling how long you'll be here. They do ride-outs all the time. I been here almost two months now, but I seen cats ride out in five weeks. But it ain't no telling when you might bounce. They go take you up to orientation in the morning, and they give you a paper to fill out. It'll ask you to list three choices of prisons to go after here. Tell 'em Cumberland Correctional, Scottsdale Correctional, and Allen Correctional. They're close/medium security, which is what they're going to class you, being you're a first-timer with four-to-fifteen—"

"Not to cut you off," I broke in, "but what you locked up for, Rob?" It had flashed through my mind that I ought to know what put him in prison if we was going to be living together in that little cell.

"I ain't got nothing but a carrying concealed weapon case. I had my Desert Eagle on me, and they cold caught me slipping with that bitch, off in the 'jects. All I got was a year."

"You short-timing it for real! Wish that's all I had was a year. . . . But yeah, man, finish what you was saying."

"Okay. We got to stay in our cells for, like, twenty-one hours a day. We get out three times to eat, and we get to go to the gym for an hour every day. You add all that time up, it equals out to about three hours out of our cell. I go to the gym sometimes, but mainly I lay back and read the library books they bring around."

"What kind of stuff you be reading?" I asked.

"Mainly Black history. I read a little bit of everything except for fiction. But I did read one novel I liked called *Children of the State* by Nicia Aiyetoro. Now I'm reading a book about Marcus Garvey. You hip to him?"

"Heard his name before, but that's about it."

"He was a Black nationalist. Owned his own steamship company, a grocery chain, and bunch of other businesses. Way back in the 1920's. When I'm done with it, you should check it out. I knew about Marcus Garvey from back in the day though, when I used to get put on punishments at home. My father and my Uncle Don used to make me read about him and about the Black Panthers and Malcolm X. You probably hip to Malcolm X, right?"

"I know about the Panthers and Malcolm, but I ain't never read anything about them. My mother named me after Malcolm X. That's where I got my first name and my middle name too. It's Xavier. She told me to see that Spike Lee movie about Malcolm X, but I never did."

We talked most of my first day in prison as a wrongfully convicted felon, and afterewards I began to think I was going to find my way through the physical and verbal confrontations that go with prison culture without too much trouble. But I wasn't so sure about dealing with the emotional side of it. Even before I stepped inside LCF I was feeling pretty damned depressed about getting nailed for something I didn't do. But that first night in the cell just depressed the fuck out of me, and I couldn't sleep. As I laid there in bed and stared up at that cement ceiling, I started to wish I'd never been born.

My life was in shambles, *and I hated it.*

Chapter Twenty-One

"When a person places the proper value on freedom, there is nothing under the sun that he will not do to acquire that freedom. . . ."

I felt a surge of adrenalin when I read that opening passage in my first library book, a week after Rob recommended it. As I think about it now, that was my first whiff of enlightenment from my namesake, the astonishing Malcolm X, who went from being a once-upon-a-time, gun-toting street hustler and convicted felon to a revered statesman and champion of human rights. As each day passed during the week it took me to read the book, I began to think more and more about gaining my own freedom. I began to ask myself questions that got more and more specific: *Why do I have to accept being caged up like an animal? Is it just because I failed to lift the massive weight of oppression the man himself put on my shoulders? How can I get enough money together to hire an attorney?* I was beginning to realize I'd been deaf, dumb, and blind during my court proceedings.

I rolled over on my side, tired as if I'd been lifting boxes all day. "I'm done, my nigga," I said to Rob, who was underneath me on his bed, also reading a book.

"You finally done? It's about time!"

"Man, that book was almost 600 pages. I ain't read something that long before. But that's some book. I ain't know Malcolm X was off-the-hook the way he was. He was dropping science on *everything!* That part where he says Black people don't even know their true language or their true names—I read that, and I was tripping."

"You got to get the Soul Brother #1 book now," Rob said.

"You talking about James Brown?"

Rob burst out laughing. "Naw, man. I ain't talking about no James Brown, you ol' get-on-the-good-foot, silly dude. I'm talking about Marcus Garvey, fam!"

"Okay, I got you now," I said with a grin. "I'm go get that one next if they got it." I laid there and thought about Malcolm X some more. "But yeah, man, I'm about to figure out how to come from up under all this bullshit."

"Come from up under what bullshit? What you talking about?"

"I'm talking about all this damn time they buried me under. I'm not accepting it, man. I shouldn't never have copped-out to none of that stupid shit in the first place. But some kind of way—on the *by any means* side—I'm go find a way to get myself a *paid* attorney. I'm coming from up under this bullshit, and that's on everything!"

"I feel you on that, fam, for real," Rob said, his voice rising. "If I was in your situation, I'd be trying to do the same thing. What the fuck a nigga look like just accepting time when they ain't even done nothing? That's crazy. And even if a motherfucker *was* guilty, they still don't got to lay down and take it. That's one of the main reasons all these prisons is full of niggas the way they are. Niggas be locked up, and then they just be accepting whatever the White man do. Just look at when you first came in here last week. All you seen was a bunch of niggas running around, acting stupid, like this some kind of game in here or something. You ain't seen none of them White boys doing that shit. You know why?"

"Why? Because they scared?"

"Naw. Some of them probably are scared shitless, but it's because they're trying to brainstorm a way out of their situation, just like you doing right now. You on the right path, fam. You got to, like my Uncle Don always be telling me, stay down for your crown."

If someone asked me to name the most significant period in my incarceration, I'd say it was when I celled with Rob. He introduced me to true knowledge, wisdom, and understanding. He knew about everything from philosophy to business, and I learned to listen every time he talked about something that was insightful. I learned about stuff like the turpentine bombing of Tulsa, Oklahoma, when that city was predominantly Black. White racists bombed it aerially in the early 1920's because they resented the financial success of what they called the Black Wall Street. I learned about people like me who got trapped in the pitch-black darkness of mental stagnation and then went on to triumph and to succeed in their own way. He told me about Elaine Brown, the Black female revolutionary who once *led* the predominantly male Black Panther Party. He told me about George Jackson, the courageous martyr and activist who wrote *Soledad Brother* and *Blood in My Eye* while he was incarcerated. I can't say I would *never* have learned about all the things he taught me in those two months, but I can say I would never have learned them *on my own* in that early stage of my incarceration.

Meeting Rob was an awakening.

Outside of talking about politics and history, Rob and me had our share of recreational conversations. We talked about cars and about getting rich. And we named about a hundred women we wanted to fuck. It made the time fly. Plus, it helped me break the spells of depression I was experiencing—especially right after mail call.

From the beginning of my incarceration, the mailman was not kind to me. Not even my mother wrote to me at LCF. It was as if everybody had just disappeared off the face of the planet. My mother was most likely shacked up somewhere, high as hell, completely oblivious to what was going on in the rest of the world. So it really wasn't a big surprise not to hear from her. It was a surprise not to hear from *anybody*. It wasn't like I had a bunch of friends, but I never thought I wouldn't receive any mail. I figured to hear from an old classmate, somebody from the recreation center, Ms. Gray, or *somebody* would have dropped me a line to say, "what's up?" But I was wrong, and after two months I realized I wouldn't be hearing from anybody for a long-ass time.

Rob and me continued our routine of politicking and kickin' it about women until he rode out to his parent institution. We exchanged I.D. numbers and promised to stay in contact. But after he left we lost contact. Like they say, it was "out of sight, out of mind."

About six weeks after Rob left, I rode out to my parent institution with thirty-five other inmates. It was the middle of June, 1994, and we left early in the morning, before the sun came up. The transport officers refused to tell us where we were headed, which made no sense to me, being we were already on the bus and on the way, secured in belly chains, shackles, and handcuffs. After six hours we pulled up to the secluded entrance of the 1,300-bed, single-cell occupancy, close/medium security Cumberland Correctional Institution.

Chapter Twenty-Two

CCI, like LCF, was located in a rural area, near the predominantly White, southern Ohio town of Portsmouth, approximately 320 miles from the city streets of Cleveland, where I grew up. The town had a few thousand people, and a lot of them made their living, directly or indirectly, through the local "prison-industrial complex." Like Woodhill, where LCF was the main employer for people who had previously worked in the steel mills, Portsmouth depended on the prison to keep its economy going. Both towns would have collapsed like card-houses in a tornado without the prisons.

But the towns had their differences too. The people in Woodhill tended to be liberal Democrats. Portsmouth was full of racist Republicans.

When I arrived at CCI and was standing in the Receiving and Delivery area waiting to be processed, I noticed every White officer--lieutenants, captains, and block officer--had a bald head and chewed tobacco. As well as I could tell, they all had tattoos: two dagger-like lightning bolts on the side of their necks. I knew they stood for a White supremacy organization, and I found out soon enough they stood for a Hitler-loving, racist, anti-Semitic National Socialist German Workers' Party, more commonly known as the Nazi Party that ruled Germany from 1934 to 1945.

It tripped me out to be in the presence of a bunch of real White supremacists, being from the hood where I never saw White people, let alone wannabe Nazis. But what really tripped me out was the fact that the racist officers were allowed to show their colors on the job. What the fuck? I mean it wasn't like they were employed by some under-the-radar car wash. These motherfuckers worked for the *state government*! They were supposed to be righteous civil servants of the state of Ohio, not some in-your-face, racist Willie Lynch overseers. I knew I was living in the U.S. of A., where slave-owning

Thomas Jefferson and George Washington are celebrated as fathers of freedom, not greed-driven profiteers. But it still surprised me to find racism being waved in everybody's face at CCI.

My country 'tis of thee, sweet land of liberty. Right.

A year had passed at CCI, when the short, fat, redneck relief officer stood in front of my cell with a stack of mail. "Are you inmate Jordan?"

"Yeah."

"State yer number," he said.

"Zero three one dash three seven five two."

He slid two letters under my door and walked away. "Ain't this a bitch," I said out loud as I picked them up and saw the "return to sender" sticker on the top one. My neighbor, Corleone, gave me a pen pal address off a list he'd ordered, and here it came back, address unknown. I tossed it on the floor and looked at the second envelope. It was from my mother, which surprised me. I'd heard from her three times since I'd been incarcerated. She promised to write once a week in her last letter three months earlier, and I was finally hearing from her again.

I stretched out to read her letter, and I shook my head at the redundancy. She was getting ready to look for a job, planning to check into drug rehab, and hoping to send me some money. I'd heard it all many times before, starting at George Junior Republic. She sounded like a broken record. But just as I was finishing up the last paragraph, I cut my eyes away to the postscript at the bottom. There was Larry's name, which got my attention. "P.S. I hope you don't get upset with me, but I'm moving back with Larry in a few weeks. Just to let you know."

I couldn't believe it. No way in the world should my mother have *thought* of moving back in with Larry after all the bullshit he put her through. He beat her ass like a drum and abandoned her when she went to prison, and after I'd damn near caught a murder rap for defending her from him she was crawling back to him like a stray dog looking for refuge. Un-fucking-believable!

I'd felt for a long time that I'd lost my mother to the fucked up world of drugs. But now she was moving back in with her tormentor, and I knew without a shadow of doubt that I'd lost her. It would be just a matter of time until something tragic happened to her. She was going to be ambushed by a "permanent pause in life," better known as *death.*

When I arrived at CCI a year earlier, I came through the door planning to use the little over $400 I still had on my account to buy myself an ounce of weed and get my hustle on. My goal was to be able to retain an attorney who was "bout it, bout it" so I could get back in court and out of prison. I thought I could cop some weed just by asking around, but I was wrong! It wasn't like TV or the movies, where drugs are easily available in prisons. CCI was as dry as the Mojave Desert. I couldn't find dope anywhere.

I found out what happened. A couple of years before I got to CCI, the Department of Rehabilitation and Corrections launched a "war on drugs" in all of its more than twenty prisons. Before that, drugs *were* everywhere. Prisoners were overdosing and dying every other week, and prison employees who were smuggling the stuff in were getting attacked by their incarcerated co-conspirators over delivery and price disputes. NBC's *Dateline* aired a story about an Ohio assistant warden who got caught smuggling in five pounds of weed, and shortly afterwards the DRC dropped the hammer on the entire system. They ransacked every cell in the state more than once. When the smoke cleared, they succeeded in almost all the prisons, including CCI. Every now and then somebody would luck out and smuggle a few joints in through the mail, but that was it.

When I realized I wasn't going to become a penitentiary drug kingpin, I threw in the towel on my cannibas ambitions and bought an overpriced 13-inch, color TV and a Sony walkman. The monotony of my first two months in CCI was unbearable, and the TV and radio broke the boredom. But they broke my account too! After I bought the electronics and a few rap tapes, I was down to $4.20. Like countless other Blacks in the system, when my account dipped below $10, I became an indigent “state baby,” an inmate whose only source of money comes from their penitentiary job salary, $9 per month. But state baby or not, I was determined to find a way to get a paid attorney.

There had to be a way.

Chapter Twenty-Three

From the start at CCI I stayed to myself, did my best to be incognito. I didn't open up to anybody except my goofy, exaggerating neighbor, Corleone. We sat at the same table during chow when I first arrived, and he gave me the rundown on the place. From there on we just got cool with one another. He was Black, in his early twenties, plus a first-time offender, so we had some things in common. But we kept our conversation sort of formal. Prison just doesn't seem to be a place where you bond and socialize wholeheartedly.

There were almost 70 inmates, mostly Black, in my cellblock, just nine of them White and two Hispanics. Most of the Blacks were old-school, repeat offenders who fucked around with the homosexuals. There were five out-of-the-closet fags in the block, and they were just about all I heard them old-school niggas talk about. They didn't talk about women or money or nothing else, just fag shit all day everyday. I didn't have anything in common with any of them. And the rest of the Blacks in my block were gangbangers. I didn't have anything against any of them, but I never hung out with Bloods or Crips or Folks or Vicelords before I came to prison, and I wasn't about to start. Being a hanger-on just wasn't my style. And as for the Whites in my block, the ones who weren't gay, they were either Skinheads or Aryan Brotherhood, and I wasn't about to associate with those racist motherfuckers.

After close to eighteen months at CCI, I began to mellow out and started thinking about my future beyond prison. I wasn't sure what direction I wanted to go, as far as making a living, but I liked the idea of owning my own business. I thought about getting out and trying to get on the roster of a semi-pro team somewhere, hoping to work my way up to the NBA. It would be a long shot, but you can't make the shot if you don't take the shot. I had a little over a year to go before I went to the Parole Board, and I was nowhere near the right frame of mind to get myself into tiptop physical shape.

At that time I still wasn't getting any mail, and I found myself fading in and out of a deep depression. One day I got so depressed I broke down and wrote a letter to my conniving ex-girlfriend Sharon. My intention was to sweet-talk the maggot bitch and get some money out of her, and maybe a few pictures of her, naked. But the heartless bitch didn't even write me back. My luck was terrible. It could be raining pussy outside, and I'd be the only one who got struck by lightning.

Although I was depressed and craved companionship, what I really craved was some *money.* I was miserable about being in prison for something I didn't do, but I was twice as miserable about being in prison with no money!

I've heard White people on TV, multi-millionaires, say they wished they weren't rich, that money had destroyed their lives. I've heard them say the more money they accumulated, the more miserable they were. But they wouldn't feel that way if they were sitting in a prison cell, penniless, serving years for something they didn't do. They would learn real quick that money is *everything* when you're a captive, entangled in a web of American injustice.

As I watched the slow cycle of the seasons from inside, the by-any-means-necessary mentality I'd felt at the beginning of my incarceration faded out of my mind. I blame a lack of self-discipline and a lack of focus. I took my eyes off the prize, as the saying goes. Instead of working on a way to escape "the belly of the beast," as I'd vowed to do, I sat around doing nothing, feeling sorry for myself. It was as though I'd fallen off a bike and instead of getting up and climbing back on the bike, I just lay there on the ground, rolling around in my own self-pity, hoping somebody would come along and give me a hand. Eventually, after six months, I saw an African proverb in a *Vibe* magazine: "Whom that is truly dying of thirst, blindly shall they certainly find a river." The more I thought about it, the more it gave me strength. Here's how I understood it: when someone is truly *dedicated* towards accomplishing something important, they *will* accomplish their goal, against any odds.

The proverb's message lifted my spirit and inspired me to "find the river." After I made up my mind to get back on my square, I didn't waste any time conjuring up a strategic plan to liberate myself.

Two weeks before the Thanks*taking* holiday, 1995, I went to the library and signed out a copy of a Cuyahoga County phonebook white pages and sat down and copied over 100 names and addresses of randomly selected people. I took the list back to my cell and drafted an introduction letter to send to everyone on my list, hoping to persuade some of them to offer me some kind of support. I stayed up all night until breakfast writing out copies of the letter and addressing stamped envelopes. I had just six stamps at the time, but my strategy was simple: mail out as many introduction letters as possible. I figured if I stayed persistent and kept mailing letters, the laws of scientific probability meant I'd find someone willing to help.

The introduction letter went like this:

> *Greetings:*
>
> *I know you must be wondering who I am. And why am I writing to you? Let me explain.*
>
> *My name is Malcolm Xavier Jordan, and I'm a 20-year-old Black male. I'm currently incarcerated at the Cumberland Correctional Institution in Portsmouth, Ohio. I'm a native of Cleveland, and in 1994 I was sent to prison for crimes (complicity to commit robbery and carrying a concealed weapon) that I didn't commit. Unfortunately, I am without the assistance of someone to support me during these trying times, which is what led me to writing this letter to you. (I obtained your name and address out of the phonebook.)*
>
> *I don't know what your feelings are towards people who are incarcerated, but I'm*

writing this letter to you in hopes that you're someone who is understanding of people like me who got caught in a web of early mistakes. So having said that, I'd like to ask if you'd be willing to become my pen pal. I think you might be able to give me some much-needed moral support. I surely would appreciate it.

I don't want to be intrusive so I'll keep this letter brief. If you do decide to write me back, feel free to ask me any questions you may have about myself or my situation.

Thank you for your time.

Sincerely,
Malcolm X. Jordan

Overall, I thought I did a pretty good job with the introduction letters. They were written in cursive, and the penmanship looked nearly flawless. I thought it would be just a matter of time before the pen pals started responding. My confidence was soaring!

Because I was living on a shoestring budget, when I received my monthly $9 prison salary, instead of buying my hygiene items and stamped envelopes from the commissary, I'd buy everything with Little Debbies through the black market. Little Debbies were a hot commodity, and a $1.25 box of Swiss Rolls traded for 10 to12 stamped envelopes on the market, which enabled me to turn seven boxes of Little Debbies from the commissary into $20 worth of black market merchandize. This is how I financed my letter writing campaign, and I sent out introduction letters at a clip of 40 to 50 per month.

Two months passed by after I began mailing the introduction letters without a single response, but I tried to stay optimistic. I knew it took time to become successful at just about anything, and I forged ahead with 40 to 50 letters per month. But after four months went by without a response, I bowed to carpal tunnel syndrome and brought the campaign to an end.

In prison, adversity can lead a person to overcome obstacles and accomplish a lot, but it can also lead a person to feel defeated and dejected, which is what I felt deep down inside—that I was gradually evolving into a loser.

I was still young, but the saga of Malcolm Xavier Jordan was a train wreck.

Chapter Twenty-Four

Shortly after 1996 rolled in, I started playing basketball four or five times a week. My love for the game had diminished since being incarcerated, but watching that year's NBA All Star game, I began to feel the old passion again. I began to play with a Black guy named Auto. He was 6 feet, 7 inches, 260 pounds, and the rumor was that he'd been recruited to play football at Ohio State. I don't know if the rumor was true, but he definitely had the size and athletic ability to play college *basketball.*

One day Auto and I were playing one-on-one. We were both very competitive, and we played hard. Auto generally came out the victor, but this day I was kicking his ass. I was up on him two games to none, and when we got ready to start a third game, he asked if I wanted to place a wager on it. We hadn't made any bets on other games, and I didn't have any money except for the monthly state pay, so I passed on the offer. Auto didn't want to take no for an answer. I guess I had bruised his ego by kicking his ass two games in a row, and he must have thought he had to win something from me to mend whatever damage I'd done.

"Let's just bet a couple of boxes of Debbies or something," he said. "It ain't nothing but a couple of dollars, my nigga."

I took a jump shot and made it, and then I paused for a brief second. "Fuck it," I shot back. "Let's play for a box a game, going to ten! Make it, take it."

"That's a bet, my nigga. Shoot the die for first."

I took a jump shot from the top of the key to determine which of us would get the opening possession. It went in, all net, and I didn't waste any time taking it to Auto. I went up on him 6-2, knocking down long-range jump shots just as I had in the first two games, while he had the ball for just one possession. I made my first three shots, and when I missed, he got the ball and backed me down underneath the rim for two quick, easy points. He let me know with his aggressive play that he was go exploit his size advantage every chance he got. When he scored the second point as easy as he did, I thought he was about to run the table on me. But when he tried backing me down for a third time, he dribbled the ball off the side of his foot, and it went out of bounds. I got the ball back and picked up where I'd left off by sinking two more mid-range jump shots. Auto tried to step up his defense, but he was so aggressive he fouled me and knocked me to the floor—three times in a row! I played through the contact, and when I hit my sixth jump shot, Auto retrieved the ball and slammed it hard on the ground. He was heated. My jump shot was all the way on, and he *knew* he couldn't stop it. After we checked up the ball he continued to play aggressive defense, but like an experienced martial artist, I used his aggressiveness against him. I knew he was go try with everything he had to block my shot, and I baited him with a perfect head fake that got him in the air. As soon as he went airborne, I drove to the hoop with two power dribbles and threw down a two-handed tomahawk dunk that would have made Charles Barkley proud.

The guys in the gym went *crazy*. I went up 7-2, but Auto thought otherwise. "Man, that's my ball up top."

Not taking him serious, I grinned. "Your ball? You must be crazy!"

"I'm serious. You traveled on that dunk, nigga."

I stopped grinning. "Traveled? Man, get the fuck out of here! Ain't nobody traveled. . . . I took *two* steps!"

Auto's entire demeanor changed, and he started walking slowly towards me with a hard look on his face. "If you only took *two* steps, then why the fuck I call travel, *dumb-ass nigga*?"

I couldn't believe what he was saying. Although we trashed each other every now and then, we never disrespected one another. I didn't know who he thought he was talking to that day. But it was go be a bunch of thunder and lightning in that gym before I let him punk me out. He just kept walking towards me. I took a step back. "I don't know why you called a travel, but if you walk up on me, I'm go show you who the dummy is."

Auto paused for a split second and sucked his teeth. "Yeah? . . . Nigga, *suck my dick*!" He grabbed his crotch.

I was less than three feet from him, and when he said that disrespect, I punched him in the mouth without even thinking. It was a hard straight left hand, and I threw it with bad intentions.

My punch caught him by surprise, and it split his lip open. But he didn't go down, and he countered with a slow, lunging overhand right that missed me. He seemed dazed from my punch, and I didn't waste any time. I moved in and hit him with another hard left that connected with the side of his chin. His legs gave way, and he stayed down, face first, until a stretcher arrived. I didn't actually get to see what happened later.

No sooner after I laid Auto out like a bed spread a bunch of officers came rushing into the gym with their PR-24 nightsticks in their hands. "Get down! Get down!" was all I heard, and I didn't waste any time getting down. I knew they wouldn't hesitate to club me senseless if I didn't, and I let them handcuff me and take me to the hole.

It was my first time in the hole, and the chaotic environment wasn't anything like the cellblocks, where you could sometimes find a little peace and quiet. Unlike those fully enclosed steel and concrete cells, the cells in the hole had old-fashioned see-through iron bars that let anybody see into your cell. And the hole was dirty as hell. The tiers smelled like the back of a garbage truck and were littered with stains of dried up feces that inmates threw at each other or at officers. This kind of biohazard warfare, called "bombing," happened so often the prison officials didn't bother to clean it up.

Because I'd gotten into a fight, I had to go in front of the Rules Infraction Board so they could determine the number of days I had to stay in the hole. The RIB panel was made up of three White male lieutenants who were supposed to give rule violators a chance to defend themselves. But just like courtrooms all over the United States, the RIB panel wasn't really interested in upholding due process, protecting the rights of the accused. The result was guilty verdicts for nearly everybody who came before them, including me.

I was one hundred percent guilty of the fighting rule infraction stated in my conduct report. But despite that, I should have been found *not guilty* because the RIB exceeded the two-week time period allowed to adjudicate my case. They heard my case 22 days after I was put in the hole, which was a violation of due process. In spite of the time violation, I was given an additional 15 days in the hole, and they told me I was lucky not to be written up for *assault* and placed in "administrative control" and kept in lockdown *indefinitely.*

I appealed my RIB conviction while I was in the hole, but I never received an answer. Somehow I thought I was about to get some justice, but I probably should have known better. I *definitely* should have known better. But I took it in stride, and before I got out of the hole I made a vow to myself to stay out of trouble and focus on my parole hearing coming up. Nothing was more important than my freedom.

I was released from the hole a week before my twenty-first birthday. Although I didn't do much celebrating about the birthday, I got some joy from a newspaper article my neighbor gave me to read when I got back to the block. It was titled "Sentencing Reform Could Free Thousands," and it explained the ramifications of the new flat-time sentencing guidelines that were supposed to be implemented on July 1, 1996, as a cost-effective measure. They were hoping to save the state millions on prison costs.

According to the article, incarcerating offenders like me for indefinite terms was fiscally irresponsible. It was crippling the state financially because of the Parole Board's unwillingness to grant thousands of paroles to inmates who served *years* beyond their parole-eligibility dates. At a whopping cost of $40,000 per year for one inmate, it didn't take a genius to see that with 47,000 inmates in Ohio, there had to be some change. Worried mainly about getting reelected, Ohio's legislators brought forth their version of radical change. They introduced new, definite sentencing guidelines, commonly known as "flatline" guidelines. Offenders sentenced under the new guidelines weren't required to go in front of the Parole Board to be released the way the rest of us were.

The flatline guidelines were going to benefit thousands of offenders once they were enacted. But they were going to help only those who committed their criminal offense on or after July 1, 1996, and according to the journalist who wrote the article, the timing "posed a potentially messy legal dilemma for the state of Ohio." The problem was the legislature's incomprehensible decision not to apply the new guidelines retroactively to all state prisoners. They created a separate, pre-July 1, 1996, class of offenders who would get disproportionately longer sentences than those sentenced under the new guidelines even if they committed identical crimes. So an offender sentenced under the older guidelines for a first-degree felony, excluding murder or murder-related offenses, would have to serve a five-to-25 year term, determined by the control freaks on the Parole Board. An offender sentenced under the new guidelines for committing the same first degree felony has to serve only a minimum of three years up to a maximum of ten, and it's determined by the trial court before the offender steps a foot inside a prison. That's a possible disparity of 22 years! The person sentenced under the new guidelines could get three years, and the person under the old guidelines could serve *a quarter of a century*!

"Messy legal dilemma" didn't get it. The thought of having to serve significantly longer on my prison sentence than somebody coming in under the new guidelines made my blood boil! In a span of just a few seconds I saw images of prison rebellion flashing through my mind. I guess my subconscious had been absorbing all the in-your-face, unjust realities of the American criminal justice system that spelled it out: "*No justice, no peace*!"

In the darkness of that article I kept reading and looking for light, some glimmer of hope that I might not have to serve the full term of my indefinite four-to-15 sentence. And then a ray of light appeared in the last paragraph: "Discussions between Governor Morgan and the chairman of the Parole Board are under way of a possible amendment to existing policies that would, if enacted, make possible the mandatory release of all old-law offenders convicted of a non-murder or murder-related criminal offense *upon serving the minimum portions of their indefinite sentences.*" Even though the article didn't provide anything definitive about the amendment, just the possibility that the old policy might be changed was enough to keep hope alive.

It was the only thing I had--the only thing thousands of other old-law offenders had if they wanted to be free.

Hope, hope, hope.

One day after my birthday I received a birthday card and a letter from my on-again-off-again mother. It caught me by surprise because she hadn't written on my previous birthday. Plus, we'd become very distant because of all the broken promises and lack of communicating. Over time, I'd just blocked her out of my mind. I know that sounds harsh, but to maintain my sanity, I had to delete all the stress from the free world and adopt a reclusive, fuck-the-world attitude. It's a sociopathic way to think, but when you're locked up in a cell the size of a parking space, you do what you have to do to make it through to the next day. It's a matter of self-preservation.

After my mother moved back in with Larry, her letters generally began with a long explanation of why she did it. I expected my birthday letter to do the same, but she threw me for a loop. She started by informing me she'd been in contact with my brother, Corey. Since I'd never seen him in person or even spoken to him on the phone, I'd practically forgotten I had a brother. But being in my crazy, wrongfully incarcerated predicament, I badly needed my morale uplifted by anything, and this was good news.

She went on to tell me my brother was getting ready to enlist in the Marines and wanted to get to know me before he did it. She mailed me his phone number and address a couple of days later, along with a much-needed $20 money order, and she told me to contact him as soon as possible. She didn't say much about herself in either letter, but I assumed she was doing okay. The average drug addict doesn't have money to give to anybody who isn't dealing drugs. So maybe she was clean.

I started to think about my brother and wonder what his life had been like with adoptive parents. *Was his family as dysfunctional as mine? Did he have any adoptive siblings? Had he ever been in jail?*

As soon as I received my brother's contact information, I got on the phone to start a long overdue relationship with him, but I wasn't able to get through to him because his phone service provider wasn't "contractually compatible" with my institution's greedy phone service provider. This was just one of the ways families and friends of hundreds of thousands of prisoners got exploited for financial gain by the great white sharks of corporate America. If my brother wanted to talk with me, he was going to have to enter into a costly financial agreement with my institution's phone service provider. For $10 to $15 he would be allowed to speak with me for twenty minutes, a call that would cost one quarter from a phone booth. With the prices folks paid to receive our collect calls from inside a correctional facility, you would think our fucking calls were buzzing over 24-karat solid gold wires.

But we are the bad guys.

After failing to contact my brother on the phone, I wrote him a six-page letter and did my best to get to know him. I told him about the time I threw the radio in the tub with Larry for beating on our mother, and I told him about all the mental lapses that led to being incarcerated for crimes I didn't commit. I let him know I wanted to meet him someday and told him even though we weren't raised up together under the same roof, we needed to have each other's back. I concluded the letter on a light note with a "plea of desperation," asking him to pass my name and address on to "one of them sexy, chocolate, South Carolina girls" so I could partake of some recreational interaction with a female because *I missed everything about a woman*. And I meant *everything*!

The next day I mailed my letter to my brother and began the anxious wait of the six to seven days it took to get a response from a letter sent by regular mail. I wasn't used to getting mail, and it was a slow, grueling, psychologically challenging process that felt like Chinese water torture. But it was good to look forward to having some form of reliable family support.

It felt to me as though I had what the people of Philadelphia were renowned for having: brotherhood.

Chapter Twenty-Five

(The Parole Board: October 1996)

After barely two decades of existence, I realized the most anticipated day of my life was my first Parole Board hearing for crimes I didn't commit.

"Good afternoon, Mr. Jordan. Have a seat." The man officiating, a Gregory Hines lookalike, spoke as I walked through the door into the raggedy, windowless conference room after six hours of waiting. I started waiting at eight in the morning, and it was two in the afternoon. "My name is Mr. Fletcher."

I sat in a wooden chair on the opposite side of the steel table from Mr. Fletcher, and I could feel my heart pounding. I was nervous as hell.

He continued. "You've been waiting a while so I'll get straight down to business with you, Mr. Jordan. I've read your file carefully, and your convictions aren't too severe in regard to the nature of the crimes you committed. Nobody was physically hurt. What concerns me is the fact that you engaged in a conspiracy to have *multiple* locations held up *at gunpoint*! Most first time offenders like you have only 'consolidated offenses' on their records. You know what I mean by that, right, when I say 'consolidated'?"

I paused and stared and slowly shook my head as though I was completely bewildered, but I knew exactly what he meant. I wanted to keep him talking about anything so I could figure out what direction he was heading. Was he leaning toward granting or denying me a parole? I figured if I heard something suggesting he planned to deny the parole I fully expected to get, I could interject *something* on my behalf that would turn the thing around.

Adjusting his Mr. Peabody-style glasses and smoothing out his preppy argyle sweater, Mr. Fletcher continued. "What I mean by consolidated offenses is when a series of crimes are committed in succession during the carrying out of a singular criminal incident. Say, a person robs a bank and during the getaway shoots an innocent bystander. That's two separate crimes, an aggravated robbery and a felonious assault. But even though there are two separate crimes, they both arose during the same single criminal incident, and they're deemed 'inclusive' to one another. By that, I mean they're one and the same. You follow me?"

I nodded. "I follow you."

"Now, with your particular situation, all of the crimes occurred at different times and in different locations. So your case file is composed of 'non-consolidated offenses,' for which the Adult Parole Authority's procedural guidelines mandate 'a continuation of incarceration' even though you have a nearly impeccable institutional record. Normally, Mr. Jordan, someone with a record as clean as yours, a first time offender—well, I wouldn't hesitate to grant parole. But with all your non-consolidated criminal offenses, I can't at the present time—"

"Hold on! Hold on for a second, Mr. Fletcher!" I cut him off, feeling panic and disbelief but knowing all I had left was my stalling tactic. He was ready to deny my parole. "When I agreed to plead in court, my attorney said I'd have a good chance of being paroled at my first hearing. Now are you telling me that according to APA guidelines I'm not even eligible to be paroled?"

"Correct, Mr. Jordan. That's exactly what I'm telling you."

"But I'm a first time offender. I ain't no *career criminal*."

"Mr. Jordan, I understand your frustration. But I don't make the policies. . . . I just do the job I'm employed to do, no more, no less."

"Mr. Fletcher, isn't it an unwritten rule that all the old-law offenders are supposed to be paroled at their first hearing since everybody reneged on the promises about reforming the Parole Board?"

He took a deep breath and let out a long, exaggerated sigh. "Mr. Jordan," he began, with a smirk that made me want to reach across the table and slap the shit out of him, "I get asked that question *every day*, and I'll just tell you what I tell everybody else: *There's no such thing as an unwritten rule with the Parole Board.* Policies govern the Board's decisions, and if a policy isn't written down in black and white, then it doesn't exist. And anything that's nonexistent has absolutely no impact on the decisions the Board renders. None whatsoever. We're aware of the disparities created by the new sentencing guidelines, but we can't do anything about it. We aren't legislators. We have to do our work within the scope of the Ohio Revised Code.

I let out a sigh of my own. "So if I'm not eligible for parole," I said, grimacing, "how much time am I getting?"

He rubbed his chin for a few seconds, looking me square in the eye. "Mr. Jordan, I'm giving you a continuance of *thirty-six months*."

I jumped out of my chair. "What?" I was shouting. "Thirty-six months! Thirty six months for what?"

Before he could try to answer my question, three fat-ass, hillbilly officers came stampeding into the room. One of them shouted, "Whoa! Sit your ass down in that chair, inmate!"

Another one asked, "Everything okay, Mr. Fletcher?"

I sat back down, and Mr. Fletcher pulled a handkerchief out of his pocket and wiped his forehead. The beads of sweat hadn't been there just a few minutes before. "Everything's fine, I reckon," he replied, sounding like a housenigga. "This hearing is over anyway, gentlemen. You can escort Mr. Jordan out when you leave."

As they led me out, I felt capable of killing *anybody* associated with law enforcement. I was seething with rage, and I wanted to bestow the pain and grief I felt onto the myriad of individuals who make a living off the modernized practices of enslaving people like me.

I know it sounds sadistic and perverse to stoop so low as to *even contemplate* taking vengeance on someone by killing them. But this sadistic mentality is cancer of the mind that grows from incarcerating innocent people in a barbaric environment populated with murderers, rapists, child molesters, and other criminals, along with all the authority-abusing employees who operate the prison. To be clear, I'm not suggesting a person is justified in committing murder because he was wrongfully incarcerated. I'm saying we're *products of our environment*. If a person is wrongfully imprisoned in an abysmal environment, embedded in misery and immoral behavior, that person is going to be psychologically scarred. The German philosopher Nietzsche said it: "If you gaze for long into an abyss, the abyss gazes into you."

After my parole hearing, I stared deep into the abysmal madness of the fucked-up legal predicament in which I was entangled. And the wretchedness and insanity of my predicament stared into me.

When I got back to my cellblock after the parole hearing that felt like a lynching, I went into my cell and sat on my bunk for five minutes without moving. I was trying to calm down. Then, out of nowhere, I jumped up off my bed, grabbed my walkman off my desk, and threw it at my back cell wall. It hit the wall and disintegrated. I felt a surge of adrenaline, and my breathing turned fast and labored. I paused and without even thinking I went for my TV. Right when I was about to pick it up, I heard my neighbor, Corleone, pounding on my wall. The noise distracted me, and I stopped.

"Malcolm!" Corleone shouted, "come to the window, man!"

I paused and then answered. "What's up man? What you want?"

"Come to the window real quick." I went to the back of my cell and cranked open my window a few inches. Corleone continued, "I know something bad happened at the Parole Board. But don't break all ya shit up, my nigga. It ain't worth it."

"It's too late, man," I said, shivering from the cool autumn air coming in the window. "I already smashed my walkman into a million pieces. But fuck it. They gave me three years, and I don't give a fuck about *nothing* no more!"

Corleone whistled. "*Three years*? How the fuck they give you three years?"

"The house-ass-nigga I went in front of was talking about how he had to give me the time because my cases were non-consolidated cases."

"I heard about that non-consolidated bullshit. . . . I don't know what to say about that. . . . That shit is ca-razy, bruh."

I let out a sigh. "You ain't gotta tell me. And what's really crazy is *I ain't even do the shit*. And they got my stupid ass to plead guilty to everything. I gotta be the biggest dummy in the world. I shouldn't never, I mean *never*, pled guilty to something I ain't do."

"You right about that, bruh."

I'd calmed down enough to know I didn't want to break my TV, but I was still pissed off. There wasn't anything I could gain by going berserk. I kicked all the broken radio pieces under my bunk, and I got in bed and went to sleep.

I woke up five hours later, hungry, and slightly confused because it wasn't dark outside. I'd missed dinner, and I didn't have anything to eat in my cell. I thought about writing a letter to my mother and brother, but I was still too shell-shocked from getting flopped by the Parole Board to do anything.

I closed my eyes and dropped into that death-like sleep that allowed me to escape the rotten world I lived in.

My brother started writing me shortly after he got my first letter. But after a couple months I think the euphoria he felt from getting to know about me wore off. He stopped answering my letters the way he did at first. He did let me know he had some "difficulties," as he called them, connected with getting ready to go in the Marines. He didn't give any specifics about the difficulties, but he did say he was going through some rough times with his girlfriend. She didn't want him to join the military. I didn't know her reasons, but I agreed with her.

To me it seemed foolish for a Black person to join the military. *What sense did it make for a Black man or woman to contract to put their life on the line for a country that trampled on their people non-stop for hundreds of years?* I posed this question to my brother in one of my letters, and he wrote back with the kind of thing you might expect from a conditioned, post-Civil Rights Black person in the U.S. "Brother," he wrote, "you need to let the past stay in the past. We live in the greatest country in the world. What's wrong with defending the country I love? It's an honor, Malcolm. It's an honor!"

To say I thought my brother's patriotic ideals and beliefs were severely flawed is an understatement. I disagreed with nearly all the social and political views he shared with me. But he was my brother so I didn't pass too much judgment on him. Anyhow, I was more concerned with trying to bond with him than with trying to reshape his beliefs. *But they sure as hell needed reshaping.*

Corresponding with my brother led me to give up a lot of the resentment I felt towards our mother. Before getting to know Corey, I assumed he would hate our mother for putting him for adoption. But it was just the opposite. He said he didn't fault her for putting him up for adoption. She did it for his sake, he said, because of her situation in those days. Seeing he had that much forgiveness in him, I felt guilty for the anger I felt for the person who gave me life. If he could forgive her, I told myself, I could forgive her too.

Two days after getting the sparks knocked out of me at the Parole Board, I finally mustered enough strength to write my mother and brother. Counting my chickens before they hatched, I'd been telling both of them I was most likely getting paroled. Now I had to turn around and tell them I got three years. Talk about egg on your face. I felt dumb as hell.

I wrote my mother first and broke the news. I wanted to tell her I felt like trying to escape because I was depressed and madder than hell. But I knew it would send her into a horrific drug binge if she believed I was sitting in a cell on the verge of losing my mind. She was drowning in drugs, and I didn't want to pour anything more on her head. In her condition she couldn't do anything to help me. So I lied and told her the Parole Board would reevaluate me in eighteen months, halfway through my three-year flop. This would have been true too if the Parole Board hadn't shelved its "halftime review" policy.

From her response I got the impression my lie produced the calming effect I hoped for. But she didn't respond to my letter until almost Christmas, and I wondered if she was really "doing okay," as she said. I had my doubts.

I gave my brother the rundown on *everything*. Told him about being blind-sided by the Parole Board. I guess I needed to vent. If I couldn't vent to my only brother, who would listen? Corey was my big brother, and as far as I was concerned, this made him morally obligated to be the one reliable person I could depend on no matter what.

Besides getting everything off my chest about the Parole Board, I told Corey for the first time that I needed a *paid* attorney to work on my case. I'd wanted to bring up the subject months earlier, but I felt apprehensive about saying anything that sounded even remotely like asking him for money. We were just getting to know each other, and I didn't want to come across as one of your typical long lost, money-hungry relatives with more greed than love in their hearts. But after getting flopped I realized how critical my situation was, and I didn't care so much how I came across.

I was hoping Corey would write me back with some ideas about getting a paid attorney some kind of way. But two weeks after I wrote, I heard from him, and he didn't mention a *single word* about anything I said. It was as if I'd never brought up the subject of needing to pay an attorney. I couldn't understand why he ignored what I wrote. Why not give me some kind of explanation? But his silence told me everything I needed to know: he wasn't going to help me get an attorney.

A couple days after realizing my brother wasn't going to help, I was able to begin thinking again about how to retain an attorney. I was sure there had to be a way, and I had to find it.

Chapter Twenty-Six

It took more than three months for me to formulate a feasible "plan of liberation." The plan was, in my opinion, pure genius, but it didn't come from the countless hours of brainstorming. It arose from a newspaper article I'd read about a controversial incident of police brutality. Three White police officers from Brownsville, Texas, were acquitted of feloniously assaulting a 20-year-old Black man they'd detained, a man named Isaiah Chambers. While he was in custody at the Brownsville Police Department, being questioned about a robbery of a credit union, he mysteriously sustained multiple head contusions and lacerations, as well as a compound fractured arm.

Chambers' injuries were life threatening, and he had to be hospitalized. He was put into a medically induced coma to treat the swelling of his brain. A nurse who knew Chamber's older sister in high school recognized him and asked about his condition. Worried, she called his sister and found that none of the family knew about his condition. When they learned what had happened to him, all hell broke loose. The comatose Chambers turned out to be the grandson of a prominent American Civil Liberties Union official, Vivian Chambers, who in the early 1970's had been married to a high-ranking member of the Black Panther party, which was then in its militant stage. When the grandmother learned what had happened to Isaiah Chambers, she called on ACLU colleagues scattered across the country. She asked them to help her call the brutal treatment of her grandson to the attention of the national media. Dozens of her colleagues bombarded newspapers and radio and TV stations with phone calls, faxes, and letters. They called for the immediate arrest and firing of all the officers connected with the incident.

Like a colony of ants, the ACLU workers got something done. Less than two weeks after the Chambers beating, the three rogue officers were on administrative leave without pay. One week later they were arrested and charged with felonious assault. All three officers entered not-guilty pleas. Shortly after that the hospitalized, bed-ridden Chambers spoke to the media. Beside him was an opportunistic spiritual advisor, the Reverend Al Sharpton. With tears streaming down his bruised face, Chambers made a brief statement about the beating. The next day he was partially quoted in a headline on the front page of *USA Today*: "They Beat Me Like a Slave." The headline, followed by his tearful account of the beating, generated massive public support in the months that followed. People all over the country were outraged by the beating of Chambers, and there was a growing consensus that the officers would be found guilty. When the highly publicized trial ended with a verdict of not guilty, pandemonium erupted all over the country. There were hundreds of arrests and property damage estimated at more than $10 million nationwide. The public reaction was described in an article about the acquittal of the BPD officers as "an explosive reaction to a verdict, rivaled by only that of the destructive, nuclear-like reaction to the verdict rendered in the infamous trial of the LAPD officers who were acquitted of all charges linked to the savage beating of Rodney King despite being caught in the act on camera."

The article about the BPD officers' acquittal was a few days old when I read it. But there had been blanket coverage days earlier, all over TV. It didn't hit me until I *read* it, the outrageous verdict. When you're locked in a cage for too long, you get desensitized. You're not likely to think about *anybody*. But when I read how the "three little pigs" got away with beating Chambers halfway to death, it triggered something in me that let me care about something again.

"How the fuck are they not guilty?" I asked myself. When I read about the reaction to the verdict in the Rodney King case, I got the idea: *set up the police by orchestrating an incident of police brutality and having it "secretly" videotaped by an undetected second party.*

"I be damn! That's it," I whispered to myself, as a surge of excitement rushed through my body. I'd just stumbled on an idea that could potentially lead to my being freed. I got so excited that I set the article on the floor and started pacing the cell, brainstorming on the best way to pull the caper off. In less than an hour I had all the details mapped out, and I jotted them down.

The plan I imagined seemed relatively simple. It required some tactical precision to covertly videotape the get-rich-quick footage. But it was a plan that could be accomplished by almost anybody with some common sense. It didn't take a rocket scientist to lure a crooked officer into beating somebody down—especially in a secluded area. And it didn't take a rocket scientist to operate a couple of tripod-mounted VCR camcorders. Everything was simple although I worried about protecting the safety of the person slotted to take the beatdown. I didn't want them to end up with their head cracked open like a coconut. But outside of that, the plan seemed almost easy.

Cashing in on setting up the police looked *real good* on paper. But there was one strategic obstacle: Finding two reliable individuals willing to partake in my skullduggery. This was the key to everything.

Instead of writing letters to strangers out in society, trying to get them to befriend me the way I'd done with my previous letter writing experiment, I decided to turn to my fellow prisoners. I knew finding the right convict to roll with me might be as tough as finding sunken treasure, but I figured the chances of finding somebody in prison to trust would be *far greater* than finding somebody to trust in society. Society has its fair share of people willing to take risks and do something illegal to make money. But people *already in prison*—they were in a class of their own. They were the elite.

After coming up with my "plan of liberation," I didn't waste much time before trying to put it in motion. I went to the library the next afternoon and sat down at a table with magazines scattered on it. As I thumbed through the magazines, I checked out the inmates in the library. There were over thirty of us, all from my cellblock. I knew nearly all their faces and most of their names. But because I mostly stayed in my cell, I barely knew anything about the character of the men behind those faces. I made some guesses after watching them for a while, and I started a list.

On the top of my list was a short, chubby Black guy in his early thirties, an inmate named Soldier from Cincinnati. He sat at the table next to mine at chow with one of his homeboys, and I'd heard him drop gems on his young homie on several subjects. Sometimes he talked about illegal stuff, sometimes about growing a business. Whatever he talked about, I could tell he was damned intelligent. And he had charisma that could rival Don King's.

Outside of knowing Soldier wasn't a dummy, I didn't know a thing about him except he was serving a life sentence for shooting somebody in the head with an AK-47 assault rifle. My idea was to try and get acquainted with him at chow and recreation—just talk for a few days—before pitching my plan. But on the same day I made my list of names at the library, I saw him eating by himself at dinner, and I said fuck it and decided to get started.

After I got my gourmet prison slop, I walked to his table. "You mind if I sit with you?" I asked.

He looked up and kind of widened his eyes. "Naw, go ahead young brotha. Have a seat. . . . Your name Malcolm?"

He caught me by surprise. "How you know my name?"

He put a spoonful of the slop they call tuna casserole in his mouth and chewed a couple times before he answered. "I'm in the same block with you, young brotha." He grinned. "I was in the gym when you got in that fight. You got my attention." He took another bite, and I waited. "*Plus*, you a real quiet guy from what I can tell. And I keep my eyes on the quiet ones. They the ones a nigga gotta watch—*for real*!"

I couldn't stop myself from smiling, and then I laughed out loud. Soldier was talking about what most prisoners believe—that quiet guys would *seriously fuck somebody up.* "Naw man," I said, stopping to butter a slice of bread. "It ain't laying like that with me. I stay to myself because I be trying to focus on getting my freedom. Shit, as a matter of fact that's what I want to holla at you about right now, for real."

Soldier stopped chewing and pointed at his own chest. "You want to holler at me?"

"Yeah."

"Well, what's up? What you talking about?"

I took a deep breath and blew out enough air to move a sailboat. "Look, I know you and me ain't never had no conversations, and I'm a complete stranger. But dig, I overheard you talking with your homeboy, and I figure you're a shrewd thinking-ass nigga from the shit I heard you talking, like that counterfeiting scam you was—"

Soldier interrupted, and his eyes were wide open. "You heard us talking about *that*?"

I nodded. "I heard it, yep."

Soldier shook his head, but I was glad to hear him laughing. "Man, you got some good motherfucking ears. But finish what you was saying."

"Yeah, I was saying you got some good ideas about how a person can make some *real* money. And I got an idea that's almost *guaranteed* to get a motherfucker paid while they still in prison. But I need somebody on the outside, somebody all-the-way thorough, to make it work. You feel me?"

He nodded. "I'm with you. I'm with you."

"Alright, then. . . . Before I go any farther, let me ask you this question: You got anybody on the street, anybody on the thorough side, who'll follow your lead whatever you tell them to do?"

Soldier pushed his half-empty tray to the side and paused. He wiped his mouth with a paper towel. "The only one I got out there like that is my little brother, Spoon. He game-

tight all the way around the board. Whatever I ask that little nigga to do, he go do it. But how about you tell me what you talking about with your idea?"

"Check this out. You seen how Rodney King got paid out there in California after them pigs jumped on him?"

"Hell-motherfucking-yeah! He sued them bitches!"

I nodded. "Right. Now imagine if somebody set up a couple of rented camcorders on tripods in a *secluded* area, and one of their dudes got the police to chase them into that *secluded* area, and then provoked the police into roughing them up while their dude with the camcorders secretly recorded it all. What you think about that?"

Soldier gave me a sinister grin. "Wait a minute," he said, and his voice was low. "You talking about *setting the police up* to jump on somebody and getting it all on tape?"

"That's what I'm talking about, my nigga."

Soldier stomped the floor and covered his mouth. "Oohh-wee! That's a winner, right there. I like it!"

Those were the words I wanted to hear, and I went straight for the jugular. "Well, shit. What's up with me and you making that shit happen?"

He was silent, watching me like he thought I might make a move. "Aw, man. . .I'd have to *seriously* think about something like that. I like the *idea*, but shit, we just meeting each other. You know what I'm saying?"

"I know what you saying, my nigga. I'm just trying to make something happen on some *real shit.* These bitches got me doing a four-to-15 for some shit I didn't even do. I'm just trying anything I can to get some money for a paid attorney. You know what *I'm* saying?"

"I feel you on that. I'm doing 33-to-life for aggravated murder, *and I did my crime.* I need all the money I can get my hands on. But regardless of how thirsty I am, I still got to be cautious when it comes to new people. It ain't like I'm saying you on some foul shit or nothing. I just need a little time to familiarize myself with you and think things over before I ask my peeps for something like this." He paused. "Give me a couple days, and I'm go holla back at you."

After pitching my idea to Soldier I walked out of the chow hall feeling confident. In due time he'd get on board with my liberation plan. He was doing way too much time to resist. He'd be a fool to pass up a chance to beat the corrupt, racist, injustice system out of tens of thousands of dollars.

I was so confident we could team up to pull my plan off that I had a hard time waiting for him to get back to me. It took him two days, but he gave me his decision in the chow hall.

I took my tray to Soldier's table, where he was sitting with his homeboy, and he introduced us. "This is my little dude, Chino," he said. "You don't mind if he chill with us, do you?"

"Naw, he cool," I said, motioning toward Chino, who was across from me on Soldier's left side. "Ya'll eat together almost every day anyway."

"You right about that. I just want to be make sure you wouldn't feel uncomfortable discussing your idea and whatnot."

Now why would Soldier think I'd feel uncomfortable talking about my illegal, conspiratorial idea in front of somebody other than him? Maybe it was the fact that I told him two days earlier that whatever we discussed about my idea was between the two of us. I wasn't trying to be talking about *nothing* in front of no Chino, Nino, or anybody else. But being I didn't want to come across as offensive, I reluctantly allowed the breach to occur. Going against my own principles, I continued the conversation.

I gave Soldier a fake grin. "Why would I be uncomfortable?" I asked as I salted my cabbage role. "Tell me what's on your mind, my nigga. I been waiting two days to hear this shit."

Soldier took a bite out his cabbage roll and started talking with his mouth full. "Alright, check this out. I like your idea. It's raw as hell—that's on everything. But what concerns me is what we go do if the police accidentally kill somebody while they beating on 'em?"

"That ain't go happen."

"*It ain't go happen*? How you know that?"

"We'll have a lookout watching everything. If the situation starts to get out of control, all we got to do is have it where the person getting roughed up give a signal on the S.O.S. side to the lookout."

"And what the lookout go do then?"

I let out a sigh. "What they go do? Shit, they go make some noise. Maybe blow a whistle or something and get the police to stop."

"What if the police chase the lookout down and beat his ass too?"

I sucked my teeth. "C'mon now, you and I we both know ain't nothing like that go jump off. You being *way* too cynical, my nigga."

Soldier chuckled. "*Cynical*, huh? That's a good word, man. I like that. But I ain't being cynical, I'm just looking at things from all the angles. When you brought it up, I was like *damn, this is one slick-ass plan.* But when I started thinking about things more in depth, shit just started popping up in my head, you know. I mean if I had my brother put this in motion, I don't want him getting caught up in no bullshit. Plus, me, him, and my boo-boo already got something lined up on the chopping block. We trying to put something down, and I just don't—"

"Hold on a second." I lowered my voice. "Who the hell is your *boo-boo*?"

Soldier started grinning from ear to ear. "Right there, man," he said, nodding to his left.

I checked out the chow hall. "Right where? I don't see no bitches."

Soldier shook his head and grinned again. "I'm talking about *Chino*, bruh."

"*Chino*," I said, still confused. "You mean to tell me your boo-boo's a *boy*?"

Before Soldier could answer, Chino snapped his fingers and jumped in. "Yeah, I'm gay. So what?" He smiled.

I was speechless. Chino was muscular and had a shaved head. Never in a million years would I have thought they were in a relationship. Knowing they were made me want to get up and walk away. I had a policy of zero tolerance for associating with homosexuals. It wasn't that I was a gay basher or anything like that. I just didn't knowingly associate with people involved in that lifestyle. It was a taboo for me. But I was hell-bent on making my get-paid-and-get-out-of-prison idea work. So I made an exception and stayed sitting at the table.

When Chino had spoken, Soldier put his palm out in front of Chino's face. "Quiet, man!" he said in a stern voice. "Ain't nobody talking to you. *Stay in your place!*"

Like a trained poodle, Chino got back in line. He didn't say another word. I couldn't believe it. Thuggish, ruggish looking niggas weren't supposed to act that way. It wasn't natural.

Soldier turned to the matter at hand. "Back to what I was saying. . . . Me and my people already got something in the works with my brother, and I don't want to chance fucking it up, gambling on something. You know what I'm saying? I'm not going into detail about what we trying to do, but it's bigger than just me. You don't fuck around so this might sound kind of crazy, but I keep shit all-the-way real in my relationship. Me and him, we're a team, man. And unlike these other clowns running round here *acting like they're a couple*, me and him don't do anything without agreeing on whatever we trying to do. . . . We discussed some of what you and me talked about, and to make a long story short, he don't really want to fuck with it. I told him—"

"Hold on a second," I said and then stopped to think. I couldn't believe what I was hearing. "You mean to say *he* got to give you the green light before you do something?"

Soldier smiled and shook his head. "It ain't like that, man. I just don't make *these* kinds of decisions without . . ."

He kept talking, trying to ease the conversation toward what he really meant to say, but I didn't hear him. I tuned him out and turned my attention to the heavy snowfall that was coming down on the window ledges outside the chow hall. I knew he was saying he didn't want to help put my plan in motion.

It was a foregone conclusion: Soldier's lack of backbone was going to thwart my efforts to bring him along. Instead of trying to make an unwilling horse drink water, I elected to concede what was inevitable and move on to the next candidate on my list.

Over the next three weeks, during library sessions and recreation periods, I set out to find a qualified accomplice. I met with all the remaining candidates on my list. I was disappointed with how things had turned out with Soldier, but I still hoped I could find somebody right on the list. My idea seemed too good to get kicked to the curb. But it turned out I'd given everybody on my list *way too much credit*. I assumed that if I was willing to take a chance at escaping a long prison sentence, somebody who'd been incarcerated years longer than me would jump at the chance to get over on the system and make some *real* money to put towards shaving some time off their sentences or at least doing their time as comfortable as possible. But the seven Black dudes on my list were, unbelievably, a bunch of *paranoid, scary motherfuckers*! When I pitched my idea to them, they all declined the offer to join up. Each one gave me a slew of scary, lame-ass excuses: *They didn't want to catch a fed case. They wasn't trying to be talking with no Secret Service. We could never get away with setting up the cops. My idea was crazy. The police were too smart to get tricked by me. We'd go to the hole forever if we got caught.*

Their excuses were lame jokes. I mean, why would the Secret Service have *anything* to do with what I was talking about? I never mentioned anything about trying to do something to the President. I just wanted to catch a crooked officer or two with their hands in a cookie jar.

As for why everybody failed to see the brilliant potential in my idea, that was a complete mystery, and it had me stressed out for a few days after getting shot down by everybody. In the midst of all the frustration, I didn't let the stress get to me, as I'd often done in the past. I was learning to roll with the punches and let the earth rotate on its axis at its own pace. I was beginning to understand that I could *influence* the outcome of a situation, but I couldn't *control* a damn thing. *Nothing.*

The only thing I was going to accomplish by dwelling on stuff I couldn't control was flying myself over the cuckoo's nest. And I refused to let myself go out like a nutcase.

After I got my mind back right, I resumed trying to reel somebody in to help me. I wasn't real optimistic anymore, though. But I was too desperate to give up and throw in the towel so I continued to take my shots here and there with a few people.

I mentioned my idea occasionally for a couple more months. But when I heard three Black dudes in the middle of the night having an all-out "Meet the Press" debate about the probability of pulling off my idea, I reversed course. I didn't even *know* any of the motherfuckers who were having the discussion, and I realized right then that I'd talked to too many people about my idea. No way could I cash in on my idea with a million people talking about it. Somebody would snitch on me for sure if it ever happened.

I should have known somebody was bound to tell their cronies everything I'd discussed with them. But I let my desperation get in the way of my common sense, and my idea was the hot topic in my block.

About a month after I pulled the plug on my idea I went back to the drawing board. But this time, like casting a net into a lake devoid of aquatic life, I came up with nothing. All I could do now was hope for the best and cross the days off my homemade calendar until I went back to the Parole Board in a couple more years.

My second parole hearing was scheduled for October 1999, and according to my calculation, I still had about 900 days to serve until my hearing date arrived—still a long way off. But in spite of having to serve a lot of time before I could be reconsidered for release, I couldn't keep from wondering what my first few days out of prison were going to be like. *Where was I going to be living when I got released? How was I going to get new clothes? Was I going to finally meet my brother for the first time? Was I going to have a chance to spend some quality time with my mother?* They seemed like normal questions for someone in my situation, but they were agonizing.

I don't know how I got to thinking about curiosity, cats, death, and that old saying: *curiosity killed the cat*. But if a cat can lose its life from being curious, then I must have been the reincarnation of one because my curiosity about what was in store for me after prison seemed to be killing me. I hated prison, and I hated uncertainty. Hated it.

Chapter Twenty-Seven

(July 1998, Eighteen Months Later)

"Try that other number at the bottom of the paper," my neighbor, Corleone, said as I walked past his cell to make a phone call for him to his new Puerto Rican girlfriend, Paula. He'd met her a few months earlier through an internet ad he'd placed.

"You talking about the number that's highlighted, right?" I yelled back over the dozens of people who were shouting back and forth throughout the block.

"Yeah?" Corleone shouted back. "And don't forget to tell her about the new visiting days this time, nigga."

Two weeks earlier Corleone got put on a 30-day phone restriction for getting into an argument with our miserable mailroom supervisor, Ms. Blackmon, a White lady in her sixties. She headed the Publication Screening Committee that screened the content of all the publications sent to prisoners and tried to make sure no prohibited material made it into our cells.

Corleone had ordered a bunch of X-rated magazines that we were allowed to have, and when they arrived, the committee refused to let Corleone get them in, claiming the magazines were too explicit. A couple of days later the committee allowed two White guys in our block to have the same magazines they refused to Corleone. After he found out the White guys got the magazines, he spotted Ms. Blackmon walking up the hallway, and he chewed her old ass out. She could have had him put in the hole, but she let him speak his mind and then had him put on phone restriction. When he found out about the phone restriction, that he wasn't going to be able to call Paula, he went off and damned near had a nervous breakdown. At first he paced the floor of his cell in silence. Then he started ranting and raving about wanting to snap Ms. Blackmon's neck. This went on for a couple hours, and after while I hit on his wall and tried to talk to him. But he ignored me. I didn't get offended. I knew too well what happens when you're really mad. He needed space, and I gave it to him.

The next morning, right after breakfast, Corleone woke me up and asked me if I'd call Paula for him. I said I would, and he gave me a piece of paper with her number on it and a list of things he wanted me to tell her and some questions to ask. I made the call, and everything seemed cool. I made some more calls for him in the following weeks. He would probably have done the same for me. The only thing about it that bothered me was when he had me asking a bunch of unimportant questions. *What was she cooking for dinner? What did she cook last night? What hairstyle was she wearing?* It just seemed crazy to make expensive phone calls to ask questions like that.

A week before Corleone was supposed to get off phone probation I made a call for him to Paula. As soon as she accepted the charges, the first thing she said was she needed Corleone to call her as soon as possible. I told her Corleone was still on phone probation and asked if she wanted me to give him a message, but she insisted he had to call her himself. As soon as I told Corleone, he started worrying, thinking the worst. Finally, he sent me back to the phone and had me press Paula to tell me what was so urgent. Come to find out, she needed to be consoled because an ex-boyfriend was harassing her over the phone. She told me she just needed to hear Corleone's voice so she could feel safe at night.

When I told Corleone what was up with Paula, he seemed calm at first. He got his cell door popped open so he could take a shower. But when he came out of his cell, he hopped his sucker-for-love ass on the phone and called Paula. I thought he was about to get put in the hole, but neither of the two officers working our block said anything to him. It looked as though he'd gotten away with it. Then two days later our block sergeant, Sgt. Harris, quietly mentioned to Corleone that "everything that glitters isn't gold." The officer who let Corleone out of his cell for a shower secretly wrote a conduct report on him for using the phone. When Sgt. Harris read the conduct report, he gave Corleone an additional 60-day phone restriction.

Corleone came unhinged. "What the fuck you mean, sixty days?" he yelled. "I had a motherfucking family emergency. I'm not doing no sixty motherfucking days!"

Sgt. Harris started yelling too. "You should have told that to the officers before you went out there and snuck your ass on the damn horn. Sixty days it is!"

Corleone kept arguing and came close to getting more days added to his phone restriction. Finally, though, he threw in the towel on the yelling and let Sgt. Harris get the last word.

Not ten seconds after Sgt. Harris walked away from his cell, Corleone knocked on the wall and told me to go to the back window. As soon as I did, he started whining and complaining about how fucked up it was. I listened for a couple minutes and then closed my window because it was unseasonably cold outside. But I wasn't really trying to hear him from the beginning because I told him before he did it not to try to call his girl until he got off restriction. He didn't want to listen to me. We were cool but I wasn't about to sit back and listen to a grown man whine about not being able to use the phone. I hadn't used it for myself for nearly two *years*. I wasn't on no phone restriction, but I might as well have been because I didn't have anybody to call. My relationship with my mother and my brother was estranged, severely. If anybody should have been whining, it was me.

A couple of hours after Corleone got his extended phone restriction, when lunch rolled around, he started talking my ear off about it as soon as we stepped out of our cells and onto the range. I couldn't escape him. "I already know, Malcolm man," he said, "I should have listened. You don't got to say nothing, my nigga. It's my fault."

I shook my head. “Hell yeah, it’s your fault! All you had to do was wait till next week. You would have been off that bullshit.”

As all of the cell doors closed on the range and everybody headed for the block exit, Corleone was smiling. “You go still make the calls for me, ain’t you?”

I paused. “Yeah, I’ll make the calls, but I’m go call two maybe three times a week at most.”

Corleone stopped walking. “Two or three times a week? What you mean?”

“Two-or-three-times-a week,” I said, holding up two fingers of my left hand and three fingers with my right. “If that ain’t good enough, then I don’t know what to tell you.”

“Malcolm, man, you on some bullshit?”

“Bullshit? How the fuck am I on bullshit?”

Corleone sucked his teeth. “Forget it, man. You don’t want to make the calls, then fuck it. I ain’t about to beg nobody to do no shit for me.”

“Hold the fuck up man. You act like I’m your motherfucking personal secretary or something. I was doing *you* a favor, nigga. I didn’t put no gun to your head and make you get on that phone. That was your choice.”

Corleone and I were trailing everybody in the line going to lunch, and I turned away from him to catch up with the rest of the block. I put some distance between us, but I could still hear him talking about the phone restriction. When we got to the chow hall line, he said something that pissed me way off. “These fake ass niggas think I need them.”

I turned around and faced Corleone. “I don’t know what’s up with this indirect bullshit you talking about,” I said quietly. “Nigga, you can’t take me on no guilt trips with you. I don’t give a fuck about your little phone restriction situation no more. You want to get mad like a little girl and call me fake after all those phone calls I made for you, then fuck you, nigga, and that bitch too.”

I barely got that last sentence out when I seen a bright flash of light in the corner of my left eye. Then the light vanished, and my consciousness was put on hold. The lame liar and sucker for love *knocked me out*! I underestimated him, and he caught me with a right hook that did some significant damage to my face, my ego, and my reputation.

I woke up in the prison infirmary, and after they took my vital signs, they took me right to the hole and stuck me in a filthy cell just a few cells down from Corleone. I was mad as hell. I wanted to base him out, but I was in too much physical pain to be yelling obscenities at him. I had a migraine headache ringing in my head like a pair of cymbals and my left eye was swollen completely shut. Corleone wasn't more than five and a half feet tall, and he weighed, maybe, 150 pounds. But he had one hell of a right hand!

Five days after I got thrown in the hole, Corleone and I went before the Rules Infraction Board. We had separate hearings, and his was before mine. They found him guilty of "fighting with or without a weapon," and he got 30 days in Disciplinary Control with a recommendation that he be placed in Administrative Control, which was unusual for somebody found guilty of a simple fight.

When I went to my RIB hearing, I expected to get found guilty even though I got knocked out. RIB found nearly everybody guilty when it came to fighting. But one of the "unhooded" RIB members shocked the hell out of me when he told me "off the record" that they knew I didn't do anything and they wanted to let me go.

Let me go? Malcolm Xavier Jordan, four-and-a-half years removed from society, the Black man doing time for crimes he didn't commit? There had to be a catch.

It was the same three White male RIB members who were on the board that found me guilty when I got in the fight with Auto, and I was supposed to believe they wanted to let me go? Something was wrong, and I found out what it was after two more minutes in my hearing: they wanted me to press *criminal charges* against Corleone.

Pressing charges against Corleone, or against anybody, wasn't an option. I wasn't a snitch, and I laughed at them. They took offense, and after telling me they knew I didn't do anything, they turned around and gave me the same disciplinary sanctions they gave Corleone: 30 days in Disciplinary Control and *a recommendation to be placed in Administrative Control.*

I couldn't believe it. I understood the 30 days in DC for refusing to cooperate with the pigs. That was the typical number of days for a fight in the chow hall. But being placed in AC? Administrative Control was reserved for *serious* cases like stabbings and rapes and attempted escapes. It wasn't a sanction for somebody who got knocked out in a one-sided fight. But as hard as I found it to believe they'd place me in AC, I remembered they'd locked me up for years for a crime I didn't do. If a regular court could do that, this kangaroo court could do whatever they wanted.

On my twenty-ninth day in the hole I went to my AC recommendation hearing. My chance to speak was in front of another all-White, three-person panel that looked like a carbon copy of the RIB panel. Maybe the peckerwoods on the two panels had different Social Security numbers, but they all had shaved heads and Nazi lightning bolts tattooed on the sides of their necks. But I went ahead and quietly told them why I shouldn't be placed in AC: I didn't have a long history of getting into fights. The conduct report for the "fight" with Corleone was just my fifth report. And the incident with Corleone didn't meet the rules infraction criteria for throwing somebody in AC. Indefinite solitary confinement for a fight? No fucking way. That's some draconian bullshit all day.

After I finished making my case for staying out of AC, they stepped out of the room and walked down the hall somewhere to take a vote. When they came back, they all had grins on their faces, and I figured they'd been down there telling racist jokes. I wasn't grinning. I was waiting to hear their verdict.

They took their time getting seated, but finally the guy in the middle spoke. "Mr. Jordan," he said, still grinning, "after considering all the factors in your file, this panel agrees *unanimously* that you should be placed in Administrative Control for an indefinite period."

I tried to hold my anger back, but I lost it. "Because I won't write a fucking statement? I knew you racist bitches was go do this bullshit!" I was shouting. "*I knew it*! . . . Fuck all you bitches! Fuck the Warden! Fuck Clinton!"

Once I lost my cool they burst into laughter. They leaned back in their chairs and laughed at me for a while, and then one of them went off to get two officers to escort me back to my cell. I wasn't making them mad, but I was entertaining them. It's a good thing I was handcuffed behind my back and chained to a steel post.

The decision to place me in AC didn't really surprise me, but it angered me. I was being punished because I wouldn't help the system tighten a noose around the neck of another Black man. And they said on my "AC Recommendation Disposition Form" that I was being placed in AC because "the fight occurred inside the Inmate Dining Room and therefore had the potential to escalate into a riot situation."

A riot situation? They didn't mention that I got knocked out at the very beginning. It was White man's justice, Black man's grief.

Corleone went to his AC recommendation hearing an hour after I went to mine. As I expected, the three laughing hyenas put his Mr. Telephoneman ass in AC too.

I had to stay in the hole for another month while all my AC placement paperwork got processed. When I finally got transferred to an AC cellblock, it was the end of September, and I had a year and a couple of weeks left to serve before I went back in front of the Parole Board. I'd been slightly optimistic that I'd be paroled at my upcoming hearing. But now that I was headed to AC I wasn't optimistic *at all*. The Parole Board didn't grant paroles to inmates in AC. It wasn't some crazy parole policy either. They just wanted to punish us, nothing else.

The only way I was going to get out at my next parole hearing was if I got out of AC before my hearing date. And the odds of that were slim to none.

Chapter Twenty-Eight

I had no clue how wild and chaotic it could be inside a cellblock until I got placed in AC. I thought I was acclimated to prison life after almost five years, but I had a lot to learn.

The morning after I was transferred, less than an hour after I arrived, I was cleaning my new cell when I heard an officer yell, "Oh, my God! Call Medical! Call Medical!" The whole block turned eerily silent, and there were no clues. Then I heard somebody say, "I think that stupid motherfucker in the shower killed his self." After that I heard the electronic gate slide open, and then a bunch of officers and nurses stampeded past my door. My cell was at one end of the range, away from all the commotion, so I couldn't see much. But word came down the range pretty fast. It turned out nobody committed suicide. It was about a self-mutilation of a guy's scrotum.

"Mutilation" and "scrotum" should never be used in the same sentence. On my first day in AC I heard them both a bunch of times from everyone who shouted about the sick-in-the-head White guy named Blevins who took a pair of toenail clippers while he was in the shower and clipped a dime-sized piece of flesh out of his scrotum right in front of our block officer while he was conducting a security check. He did it in front of the officer so the officer would get him medical attention as soon as possible. Blevins wasn't worried about medical attention though. He wanted the team of first-responder nurses, all females, to rush to the scene and treat his bleeding scrotum. He wanted them touching his genitals while they treated his injury.

Old man Blevins' strategy for tricking the nurses into sexually pleasuring him was so bizarre it could have been featured in the movie *Silence of the Lambs*. But it didn't measure up to the craziness of the "bombing" incidents in AC when inmates handled their beefs by throwing liquefied feces on their foes.

I'd heard stories of bombing years earlier, but I'd never been around when it happened. I hated smelling my own shit, and I definitely didn't want to smell anyone else's. On my second day in AC, though, the range porter, and older Black guy in his fifties called Rebel, bombed out a White guy three cells from me for calling him a *stupid ass nigger*. I'd just finished eating dinner and was standing in front of my sink at the back of my cell, just about to wash my hands, when I heard the racial-slur-spewing White guy holler at the top of his lungs: "HE THROWING SHIT ON ME, OFFICER, OFFICER!" I grabbed a makeshift mirror and rushed to the front of my cell to see what was happening. As soon as I positioned my mirror in my cell door, I caught a whiff of Rebel's weaponry, and I nearly threw up. I covered my mouth and nose with my hand and ran to the back of my cell, grabbed a towel and covered my face, trying not to catch another whiff of the doo-doo brown. But there was no way to escape it.

Rebel threw about twenty Styrofoam cups of shit that lit the block up like Christmas lights in the suburbs. And I was mad as hell! But when I saw the White guy walk past my cell, heading for the shower, I couldn't be mad anymore. Rebel slung so much shit on that dude, I felt grateful he didn't sling any on me—*and I didn't even know Rebel.* The White dude had shit dripping off his face and out of his hair, and it was splattered all over his white jumpsuit, making him look like a dingy Dalmatian. He was an ugly sight to see.

One thing I learned from Rebel's offensive was he wasn't to be fucked with when it came to biological warfare. *He was the truth!*

Except for having to watch somebody get bombed out and having somebody else mutilate *his own scrotum*, I made the transition into my new environment pretty well. It was the first week of November 1998, when I had been in AC for about six weeks. My main problem was having to listen to my loud-mouth, fat neighbor, Matt, try to sing rock-and-roll at the top of his lungs in the middle of the night. The other thing was I didn't get the full amount of my monthly $9 prison salary. It automatically got slashed in half because I was in Administrative Control.

Matt's singing irritated me because it woke me every night. But having to survive on a measly $4.50 for an entire month was a motherfucker too. I spent every penny on personal hygiene—soap, toothpaste, deodorant, lotion—but I never had enough money to buy enough to make it through a full month. If I bought enough soap to last the month, it meant I had to come up short on something else. I couldn't go without toothpaste or soap so I alternated taking the hit with my deodorant and lotion.

Not having enough deodorant wasn't really that bad because I could use soap to wash away odor. But not having enough lotion to keep my skin moisturized could drive me crazy. After I got out of the shower, my skin would dry up and crack like old concrete. It had me itching and scratching like I had chickenpox. I couldn't do a thing about it until I went back to the commissary. I tried using butter from my food tray, but it made me itch even more and had me smelling like a popcorn concession stand. I left the butter alone and rolled with the itching and scratching.

After I settled in my AC block, with the New Years holiday coming up, I decided to get a head start on my New Year's resolution: an exercise regimen with 500 pushup every other day until I went home. I was on my second day of working out, finishing up on my last few sets before lunch, when I heard the cell door next to mine get buzzed open. Nobody was in there so I figured I was finally getting another neighbor. I ground out one more pushup and jumped up to grab my mirror so I could see who was coming my way.

I still wasn't feeling much more sociable than I had through any of my incarceration, but the day-to-day solitary confinement in AC made me want to interact with someone. I couldn't stand the sound of Matt's voice, and I'd never tried to talk with him. But the idea of getting a neighbor seemed appealing as long as he wasn't on any bullshit. I didn't want a shit-slinger or another Elvis wannabe for a neighbor, but I was ready to talk.

As I angled my mirror out of my cell bars and looked up the range, I saw a White, pig-faced officer escorting a shackled and handcuffed, older Black inmate up the range toward me. The new guy was bald with a thick, bushy beard, full of gray hair. He looked to be in his late fifties or early sixties, and I think he spotted my mirror as he arrived at the cell.

No sooner had he got his handcuffs and shackles off than he pounded on my wall.

"Yeah, what's up?" I said.

"Who is that over there?" he shouted.

"My name is Malcolm," I said, remembering that I might have seen a hearing aid when I was looking in my mirror at him.

His voice got louder. "Malcolm? You the guy who worked in the warehouse?"

"Naw. Ain't never worked in the warehouse before."

"Okay. Thought you were the guy I used to buy laundry detergent from. Hey, you wouldn't happen to have a couple of matches over there that you could spare?

"Nope. I don't even smoke old-school. If I had some though, I'd rush 'em to you."

"Thanks anyhow. You can call me Deathrow. That's what I go by."

I wasn't sure I'd heard him right. Did you say *Deathrow?*"

"Yeah, that's right. Just like the name of that bee-bop record label Snoopy Doggy Dogg used to be on. You hip to him, ain't you?"

Bee-bop? *Snoopy Doggy Dogg?* I had to work to keep from laughing. He was saying *bee-bop* for *hip-hop* and *Snoopy*

Doggy Dogg for *Snoop Doggy Dogg*. "Yeah," I said, "I'm hip to him. What I want to know is how did *you* get hip to him?"

"Everybody know who that nigga is, shit. We used to listen to that boy everyday when I was on the row."

"The *row*! Wait a minute," I said. "You mean to tell me you actually been on death row?"

He let out a chuckle. "Man, that's how I got my name, *Deathrow*."

Deathrow's government name was Arthur Henry Manningham. He was born in 1938 in Flint, Michigan, and moved to Cincinnati with his parents and two sisters when he was seven. He grew up fast in that segregated city that had a reputation for burning crosses, but he also was the first person from his family to graduate from high school. Then he set out, he said, to capture the "American Dream." He criss-crossed Ohio working tedious jobs for low wages. But after almost a decade of working in fish markets, juke joints, and car washes, he traded it in for a uniform from the U.S. Army. That move led him to lining his pockets with some dead presidents, he said, but it also led his Black ass across the Pacific Ocean and into the jungles of Vietnam. After a few months of seeing body bags stack up, he realized he wasn't cut out for the duty he'd signed up for.

Private First Class Arthur Manningham decided to get himself out of harm's way by travelling down a well-traveled road taken by soldiers who want to lay their weapons down: he shot himself in the leg and reported the incident as an "accidental discharge." Within days he was back stateside, enjoying the amenities of a VA hospital. Everything had gone as planned except he did some serious damage to his leg. He had broken his tibia bone and done some serious ligament damage that his doctors said was going to take at least a year to heal. While he was absorbing this news, he met Vera Angstrom, his Scandinavian physical therapist, and then he began to hope his leg didn't heal too quickly. She was tall and curvaceous, and he immediately realized *he was in love with her*. He must have done something right during his months of therapy because a few weeks before he was supposed to be discharged from the hospital, he asked her to marry him, and she agreed.

After he left the hospital in California, they moved to Elyria, Ohio, for six months before heading to Arthur's hometown, Cincinnati. And in the summer of 1970 they were married in a little church that was only a stone's throw from a building where the Ku Klux Klan once gathered for monthly meetings.

Arthur and Vera were inseparable. They sometimes had sex as often as three or four time a day, and this marital bliss lasted for more than ten years. It was the winter of 1982 when Arthur began to suspect that something was wrong because Vera was reluctant to have sex with him. She had headaches or was too tired, and all at once Arthur found himself begging just to have sex *once a week*. Overnight, her libido seemed to be gone. He was sure if she wasn't setting the goods out to him, she had to be setting the goods out to somebody else, but he had no proof. Winter turned to spring, and nothing changed, but still he had no proof.

Then came Easter Sunday, and Vera wanted to go to church for the first time in three years. Halfway through the service, she excused herself to go downstairs and help with the post-service refreshments for the Easter crowd. Later Arthur went downstairs to the bathroom, and as he approached the Men's room, he passed a utility closet and heard a loud thud from inside. He stopped and listened, and when there was no other sound, he backtracked and put his ear against the closed door. Now he heard the unmistakable sound of a woman moaning ecstatically. He figured a couple of horny youngsters had gone into the closet to have sex, and he grinned and pounded on the door. When there was only silence, he yanked the door open.

Vera wasn't setting up refreshments in the kitchen. She was almost undressed, her pantyhose around her ankles, and the closet smelled of sex and body fragrance. An older White guy with his pants down had lipstick all over his face. No one said a word, and the silence was eerie. Finally, Arthur slammed the door in their faces. The White guy yelled something, but Arthur ignored it and headed to the bathroom. From there, he left the church and headed for the parking lot to go home.

As he backed out of his parking place, Vera came running. She was crying, and she tried to get in the car. The doors were locked. She jumped in front of their Chevy Caprice and refused to move. Arthur blew his horn twice, but she refused to move so he stepped on the accelerator and knocked her down. According to the court records, he then drove over her body sixteen times before he headed for home. One year later, an all-White Hamilton County jury, seven women and five men, found Arthur Manningham guilty of aggravated murder. A month later, a White, 72 year old judge, Bernard Rutherford, imposed a death sentence. Even for Hamilton County, it was a bit of a surprise: a Vietnam veteran, a first-time offender, and a death sentence.

Ten years later, Arthur's death sentence might have attracted the attention of some anti-death penalty organizations, but in 1983 executions didn't seem to shock the moral consciences of people in Ohio. Black men who killed White women were fair game. Arthur was transferred from the Hamilton County Jail to a cell on death row in the infamous Southern Ohio Correctional Facility in Lucasville, where he began a sentence that was meant not to rehabilitate him but to erase him from the earth.

Arthur came through his cell door in Lucasville *determined* not to die at the hands of the state of Ohio. He knew nothing about the appeal process, but he read every book about law he could get his hands on. He had a court-appointed attorney for the appeal, but he knew that wasn't enough. His life was on the line, not his attorney's. One thing he'd learned in Vietnam was that nobody but Arthur himself was going to watch out for him when his life was on the line.

Eight years after he picked up his first legal book and got involved in his appellate process, Arthur read an article in a *Jet* magazine that turned out to be important. It was called "The Klan and Its Political Ties," and he found the stories of two prominent politicians from Kentucky who had the same family name as Judge Bernard Rutherford. They were Republican Congressmen Dale Rutherford and Preston A. Rutherford, both longstanding members of the Ku Klux Klan. As their names kept appearing in the article, Arthur began to wonder if these sheet-and-pillowcase-wearing cousins could be related to his trial judge. He tore the article out of the magazine and mailed it to Clive Martin, his attorney. And he asked him to find out.

It took more than a week, but the news was good. Not only were they second cousins with close family ties, but the twenty page report Martin got from his firm's Investigation Division said in the late 1960's the two Kentucky Rutherford cousins used a Klan front organization to funnel tens of thousands of dollars into Bernard Rutherford's unsuccessful campaign to be mayor of Dayton. It was a discovery that could still be used in Arthur Manningham's appellate process. The fact that Judge Rutherford had a financial connection with the KKK didn't automatically entitle Arthur to statutory relief, but during his 1983 trial, his octogenarian attorney, Vernon Fremont, a White man, had raised numerous claims of *racial bias*. His idea was this: if his client was convicted of murdering a White woman, he could use all his on-the-record racial bias objections in an appeal to get the conviction overturned on a technicality. It was a long shot, but a White-on-Black murder conviction in Hamilton County called for desperate measures, and finding Judge Rutherford's connection with the KKK was a big break.

Fourteen months after that discovery, they won a new trial on the grounds that Judge Rutherford had been racially biased against Arthur from the moment he began to preside in the trial. Arthur asked Clive Martin to negotiate a plea-bargain that got him off death row, but the district attorney refused to budge. She was willing to discuss what Arthur wanted to eat for his last meal after they re-convicted him, but that was all.

Three months later, Arthur got the outcome he'd wanted all along: *life with eligibility for parole after 30 years.* It wasn't a sure thing for another three years because the district attorney appealed the court's ruling, almost as if she was the one trying to get off death row. But in the winter of 1996, Ohio's Supreme Court upheld the lower court's ruling. After thirteen years inside the roach-infested, windowless cell on death row, Arthur Manningham, now 58 years old, got his death sentence commuted. Exactly one week after the ruling, he was transferred to the Cumberland Correctional Institution. Two days later, while he was getting acquainted with some of the younger prisoners, Arthur was tagged with the nickname *Deathrow*. He wasn't fond of the nickname, but after hearing it for two weeks from practically everyone in the cellblock, he accepted it.

Chapter Twenty-Nine

The day after Deathrow moved next door to me, I asked if he had anything good to read. I was bored out of my mind and needed something to do other than exercising. He passed me over a book by Frantz Fanon called *The Wretched of the Earth.* Plus, he gave me a stack of anti-death penalty newsletters called *The Abolitionist.* I was glancing through the newsletters when I spotted a headline that got my attention:

Ohio's Death Row "Volunteer"
Mario Sanchez: "Pull the Switch"

I was pretty sure I recognized Mario Sanchez. He was the younger brother of Kandi Sanchez, my back-in-the-day girlfriend when we were both in the Children's Mental Health Ward right after I tried to kill my mother's abusive boyfriend.

I decided to ask Deathrow if he knew anything about it. "Hey, Deathrow, let me ask you something real quick."

"Give me a second," he answered. "I got to take a leak *real quick.*" I laughed and he didn't take long. "Here I go, youngster. What you need?"

"I just seen a headline in one of your newsletters about a guy named Mario Sanchez. If I'm understanding this correctly, he's volunteering to be executed. I might know this dude's sister. You know who I'm talking about?"

"I know *exactly* who you talking about. We was in the same block right before I got my case overturned. Mario caught his case in 1994 up there in Cleveland where you're from." I'd been hoping Mario in the newsletter was a different Mario, but when Deathrow said he caught his case in Cleveland, I was pretty sure it was Kandi's brother. "He got railroaded," Deathrow went on, "real bad, too! His sister committed suicide and everything behind his case, it was—"

I cut him off. "Suicide? Was his sister's name Kandi?"

Deathrow snapped his fingers real loud. "That's it, youngster! Kandi! It sure is."

I ran my hand through my nappy, uncombed hair. I couldn't believe it. "Are you serious, man?"

"I wouldn't kid with you about nobody killing theirself, youngster. That's definitely her name. I didn't remember it, but when you said it, I knew it was Kandi."

"When did she kill herself? And what did her brother's case have to do with it? Give me the whole rundown. I didn't read the article yet."

"It's a crazy case, youngster. I'm go try to tell you. . . . But they say Mario molested and killed a five-year-old girl his sister was babysitting. That's a bunch of bull because Mario and a couple of his little buddies were at the park shooting craps when the police said the crime happened. His sister, Kandi, she was watching at the apartment where she and Mario lived in the projects--somewhere on the West Side, I think. What happened was that Kandi, instead of watching the little girl like she was supposed to be doing, she left her by herself in the apartment and took her hot tail down the street to some older guy's house. She stayed with him for, like, two hours. When she finally took her ass back home and walked through the door she hadn't even locked, she found the little girl naked and dead on the kitchen floor. Strangled. She called 911, and when the police came, Mario popped his ass up on the set while they were questioning her. They asked him some questions too, but that was it."

"Wait a minute," I said. "You mean to tell me they didn't arrest him?"

Deathrow coughed out something like a laugh. "For what? They ain't have nothing on that boy. Shit, the only person they arrested then was his sister. They took her fast ass in on some kind of child neglect charge. Mario didn't get arrested until a week later."

"What they have on him then?"

"They claimed they found no traces of foreign DNA inside the little girl. But her private area was bloodied so they knew she got molested so they decided whoever raped that little girl wore a condom. They went back to Mario and his sister's apartment with a search warrant, and they pretty much tore it apart."

"Anybody there when they was searching?"

"Yeah, Mario was." Deathrow paused. "So they tore the place up, and you're not going to believe this, but they found a small box of condoms in Mario's bedroom, and they arrested him. They claimed he used the condoms to rape the little girl."

"So you telling me they got Mario on death row, and a fucking box of condoms is their evidence?"

"That's it. The condoms and some coerced statements from his little buddies who told them first time around he was at the park shooting dice."

I couldn't get it through my head. "If his case is that shallow, why in hell did he give up his appeals? Why he volunteer to get executed?"

Deathrow was silent for a while. "Mario don't *really* want to get executed," he said finally. "He trying to generate some publicity. He trying to get people with some kind of political clout to give him a hand. Me personally, ain't no way I'd try some shit like that, but hey, it might work for him. He be getting in them newsletters all the time so he's getting *somebody's* attention. I just hope it works out because those racist-ass Yankees will sho-nuff kill him."

"You ain't lying!" I said. "But dig, you still ain't told me how his sister killed herself."

"I'm coming to that right now. . . . Yeah youngster, a couple weeks after they found Mario guilty, his sister's old boyfriend come and found her in the bathtub with both her wrists slit."

When Deathrow said that, I flashed back to 1986 in the CMH Ward, when Kandi told me about trying to kill herself, and I couldn't get my head around that kind of pain. Sitting on my bunk and knowing she'd taken herself out of the game, I still couldn't make any sense of it. That night I cried for the first time in years. I guess I was crying for Kandi and for

Mario, for my mother and brother and myself. Maybe I was crying for the whole fucking world.

I thought being in prison for something I didn't do was the most fucked up travesty of justice that ever happened until Deathrow told me about Mario. Then I started to feel guilty for complaining. It bothered me every day, waking up inside a cell, doing time for something I didn't do, but compared with getting executed for something you didn't do, it felt like nothing.

So I decided to write Mario a letter, offer him some kind of moral support. I didn't know what to say. For one thing, I'd never corresponded with somebody who was sentenced to death. But after I stared at a blank sheet of paper for a long time, I came up with something:

December 16, 1998

Comrade Mario,

You are probably wondering who I am and what this letter's about.

My name is Malcolm Xavier Jordan. I'm a 23 year old African American from Cleveland, and I'm currently incarcerated at the CCI prison in Portsmouth. Recently, I was placed in Administrative Control, and a couple of days ago an old-school dude named Arthur Manningham (a.k.a. Deathrow) who was on the row with you got moved next door to me. We started talking, and he let me read some of those newsletters, ***The Abolitionist****. That's where I seen your name in a headline and got to wondering if you were the Mario Sanchez I was thinking of. So I asked Deathrow if he knew you. He said he met you right before he got his case overturned, and he found out how them pigs railroaded you. Plus, he told me about the tragedy with your sister. He didn't say your* *sister's name at first, but I asked him if it was Kandi. When he told me it was Kandi, I knew you were the Mario I was thinking about.*

You and me have never crossed paths, but I know your name because Kandi and I were in the Children's Mental Health Ward together when we were kids. We were close back then, and we kicked it every day. Your sister had a real good heart, man. She used to paint cartoon posters for the little kids with cancer—the kids in the Ronald McDonald House. She had "trust issues" with damn near everybody else when we were in the CMH Ward, but I'm here to tell you—and I'm sure you already know this—your sister was very fond of you. She had a smile on her face when she talked about you, and that was pretty much every day. So when I seen your name in that newsletter headline, I recognized it off-the-rip. And when Deathrow told me about your case and what happened to your sister, may she rest in peace, I had to write you, bruh.

I'm a complete stranger to you, and you got far more important things to be doing than writing letters to strangers. But I want you to know if you write me back and stay in contact with me, when I get out—and hopefully it's next year, in October—I'll work to get your name cleared. I got jammed up myself for some crazy bullshit I didn't do, robbing gas stations, so I definitely feel your pain, homeboy, to the utmost. I hate this foul-ass system with a passion, and I'm down for getting some payback on these pigs. Anytime. Anywhere.

I'm about to get this letter in the mail. But like I said, get back at me, and let me know

> *what's up. I'm go close on that note. Keep your head up and stay strong. Peace.*
>
> *A Brother in the Struggle,*
> *Malcolm X. Jordan*

After I finished my letter, I sat and thought about the reality of being on death row, hanging in the balance, knowing every day you're one step closer to getting murdered by the government. It had to be excruciating psychological torture, waking up every day in your cell knowing sooner or later someone was going to show up to escort you to the death chamber so they could either send a lethal surge of electricity through you or flood your veins with a lethal concoction of pentathol, tubocurarine, and potassium chloride.

Execution scholars around the United States decided lethal injection was "the most humane form of capital punishment." I had trouble getting into that "humane" idea when I imagined somebody showing up at my cell to take me to the death chamber. I was go be dead at the end of the day whether they hanged me or cut off my head or shot me up with potassium chloride. I'd pay some attention to whether the governor was planning to grant me a stay, but that "humane" shit wouldn't mean a thing. Living, not dying, is the only thing that would matter to me.

Thinking about Mario's reality, I was glad I didn't have to deal with the daily psychological torment of waiting for them to come and get me.

New Year's Day in 1999 was different from my four previous holidays in prison because I got drunk with Deathrow off a gallon of his homemade tomato "hooch." I was reluctant at first because I got pretty sick a few years before from drinking a quart of tainted hooch. But I decided to give Deathrow's tomato hooch a try, and I'm glad I did. It was powerful enough to start an engine, *straight firewater.* I got down about ten cups out of the gallon, but I got to the place where I wanted to be. It was a good buzz. Once I felt the endorphins or whatever, the soothing effects running through my veins, I felt like a new man. I wasn't stressed or depressed about anything. But I wasn't necessarily overflowing with happiness either. I was just in a good place, a really good place.

Despite the doubts I had about getting paroled, beginning the year in high spirits just somehow made me more optimistic about going back to the Parole Board. I figured I'd had so many bad breaks that maybe it was time for something to work out right.

Chapter Thirty

Three weeks after celebrating the arrival of 1999, just after lunch, I heard my block officer, fat Brandt, yell from the bullpen, "Jordan, git ready! Somebody wanna see ya. I'll be up to git ya."

It made no sense. I hadn't done anything wrong. But I quickly got dressed.

After while Brandt waddled his tobacco-chewing self up to my cell, cuffed my hands behind my back, and walked me over to the block's unit conference room next to the bullpen. The room was empty except for a bunch of mismatched chairs and the metal conference table. He waved me into the windowless room and told me to sit down. Then he left and closed the door. I had no idea what was up, but I sat there until an old, frail White man in a three-piece suit, dark and brown and polyester, came through the door.

"Mr. Jordan?" He looked at me, and I nodded. "My name is Chaplain Norman. How are you doing today?"

"I'm doing okay," I said. "But I'm wondering what's this about?"

The chaplain took a seat next to mine and adjusted his necktie. "I have to tell you something, son, that's going to be difficult to hear. You need to be strong right now."

"What?" My muscles tensed, and I knew the answer.

The chaplain reached over and put his hand on my shoulder. "The warden called me an hour ago to say a gentleman by the name of Larry Shelton contacted the prison this morning. Your mother, Angela Jordan, was pronounced dead late yesterday—dead from an apparent drug overdose."

As soon as he said she died of an overdose, I jerked my shoulder away. I didn't want anybody touching me or trying to talk to me. I felt like crying, but I guess I'd been inside too long, and crying for Kandi was all I could do. I couldn't shed a tear for my own mother! I wanted to, but I couldn't. All I could do was stare at the floor and let my mind roam. Nowhere. It caught me off guard, but it didn't really surprise me. I knew the lives of people hooked on drugs, especially cocaine and heroin, didn't usually turn out well, and my mother had been getting high since the Afro was in style. I knew it was just a matter of time until her number came up. When I realized my visitor was a man of the cloth, I knew my mother or my brother had died. So what the chaplain told me was no revelation. It was a confirmation.

Three days later I got a letter from my brother. It had been almost two years, and I'd given up on him when he didn't answer my letters. I had mixed emotions about hearing from him. I was mad at him for leaving me for dead because he knew I was in prison for some bullshit I didn't do. Plus, he knew I didn't have anybody supporting me. And he treated me like a stranger. But I appreciated his reaching out to me when I was mourning. It wasn't easy mourning in a cell.

My brother's letter didn't mention anything about trying to get me out, but it did include a dark chapter in our mother's life, something she'd kept hidden from me. It turned out, my brother said, when she was nineteen years old, a junkie she was shooting up with raped her in an abandoned apartment building. She got pregnant, and six months later she gave birth prematurely to her second-born son, to me.

After I read I was conceived when our mother was raped, a dark dreariness ran through my body. All my life I'd bugged her to tell me about my father, and she had refused. And it made perfect sense now. She'd been protecting me. She was doing what she thought was in my best interest. Knowing this made me feel a little better. Angela Marie Jordan was a fighter! She was courageous.

Her funeral was scheduled for one week after she died so I had four days. I'd been to just one funeral. It was for an old lady I didn't even know, and it wasn't anything I'd want to see again. But I definitely wanted to attend my mother's funeral. I hadn't been in her physical presence for almost five years and hadn't been given a picture of her in over three. So I wanted to see her *one last time.* Prisoners didn't have an automatic right to attend any funeral, but it was customary to let prisoners attend the funeral of an immediate family member. The decision was made by the Deputy Warden of Operation, and the chaplain said if a prisoner didn't have a history of trying to escape, the DWO would usually let them attend a funeral of a loved one. I didn't have anything in my record about escaping so it looked good.

After getting rode out to prison in 1994, I never imagined the next time I returned to Cleveland would be to attend my mother's funeral. I thought for sure the next time I saw the Cleveland skyline I'd be sitting in the front of a Greyhound with my seat reclined, smiling. But it looked as though I'd be inside a prison transport van, in handcuffs and leg irons.

Two days before the funeral at mail-call I got a typed communication from the DWO:

1-26-99

Dear Mr. Jordan:

This office is in receipt of a request for an inmate "bereavement leave of absence," made on your behalf by Mr. Lawrence Shelton of Cleveland, Ohio, in regard to the recent death of your mother, the late Ms. Angela Jordan.

Please be advised that, per Mr. Shelton's request, I have reviewed your institutional file to aid me in making a fair determination on whether your behavior meets the criteria for being granted bereavement privilege. I found nothing to suggest that you are a threat to escape. However, you are presently in Administrative Control for a serious rule infraction ("fighting with or without a weapon"). As you are fully aware, the

Administrative Control Committee determined that your behavior, at this time, poses a threat to the orderly operation of the institution. For this reason, and this reason alone, I cannot grant the privilege of bereavement leave.

I am terribly sorry that I must deny you the privilege of attending your mother's funeral, but your behavior does not warrant such a privilege at this time.

Sincerely,
E. Joseph
Deputy Warden of Operations

When I finished reading the DWO's letter, I balled up the paper and tried to throw it through the back of my cell wall. I couldn't believe the peckerwood had actually denied me the opportunity to be in the presence of my mother for one last time before she got buried. If I could have gotten my hands around his neck, I could have strangled him. He wouldn't have had to worry about being, as he said, "terribly sorry" about anything ever again. While he was gasping for air and semi-conscious, I would have made him regret the day he filled out the application to work in a prison. But I was locked in a cell with no chance to get my hands on his neck. Worse, I was locked in a cell in an administrative control unit, and I wasn't a threat to anyone.

Although I couldn't take my anger out on the DWO, I did take it out on *something*. As soon as I threw the balled up piece of paper the heartless DWO had mailed to me, I bolted to the back of my cell and started kicking the stainless steel sink mounted on the wall. I kicked over and over again. I was so enraged I thought I could kick the sink off the wall. It didn't budge an inch.

While I was kicking my sink like a deranged maniac, I heard my neighbor, Deathrow, pounding on my wall, and I stopped kicking to see what he wanted. "What's up, man?" I shouted.

"Hold on, young fella," Deathrow shot back in his aged and raspy voice. "I'm trying to see if you're okay over there. I know you got things on your mind, but don't take it out on me, youngster. Take a couple of deep breaths and then tell me what's going on."

I tried the deep breaths and walked up to the front of my cell. I was still enraged, but I apologized. "That was my fault, snapping at you, Deathrow. That bitch-ass Deputy Warden denied my shit to go to my mother's funeral."

"My God!" Deathrow shouted. "Are you serious?"

"Hell yeah, I'm serious. That racist bitch said I couldn't go to the funeral because I'm in AC."

"AC? Man, I seen 'em let people that was on the row go to funerals. If they can go, you can go too!"

I didn't say anything for a while, just shook my head.

"Deathrow, man, I swear on a stack of fucking Bibles, whenever I get out of here, I'm coming back down with a machine gun, and I'm go try to kill every last one of these pigs!"

"Don't talk like that, youngster."

"Talk like what?" I said. "I ain't even supposed to be in prison right now. And here it is, these bitches got the audacity to tell me I can't even go to my own mother's funeral? Man, *fuck all these bitches*!"

My mental state began to deteriorate that day. I stopped taking showers, combing my hair, and brushing my teeth. I was submitting to the dark prison-within-a-prison that trapped my mind. This dysfunctional mental state lasted for about a month. Before I lapsed into purgatory, I'd been hoping to get another letter from my brother, Corey. He'd told me in his last letter that he was going to catch a flight from South Carolina to Cleveland to attend our mother's funeral. Being that I couldn't get to the funeral, I assumed he'd come to visit me before he headed south again. But I never heard from him, and that made me let go over everything. I even stopped talking to Deathrow for a couple weeks.

While I was living like a crazed Viking, I got an unexpected letter from Mario. I'd written to him two months earlier, and his letter helped me get back on my square and regain my sanity. His letter humbled me. It practically made me feel guilty about mourning my mother's death. It was written immaculately, with perfect penmanship:

February 15, 1999

Dear Brother Malcolm,

I received your letter a while ago and I apologize for taking so long to write you back. Normally, I respond to all letters within a couple of days instead of a couple of months. I've been so busy working on my case, however, that I haven't had energy for anything else. My case is kind of high profile, and with all the publicity I've been fortunate to win over the hearts and minds of a few good people. But even though I've got some people in my corner now, I realize I don't have the kind of support that could force the powers-that-be to halt my execution or overturn my conviction like, say, the international supporters of Mumia Abu-Jamal probably could. So I have to put forth my best effort towards getting off death row. If I don't, these ruthless Ohioans won't hesitate to kill me. I write at least 3 to 5 letters to newspapers and politicians every day!

When I read in your letter that you and my sister were friends, I was kind of shocked. Growing up, man, my sister didn't make friends with nobody! She was real quiet and observant, and she just kept to herself. Me and her got split up for a few years after she went to the mental health hospital. The next time I seen her, she was way more of a sociable person. I say all this, though, to say Kandi must have really, really liked you back then if she embraced you as a friend.

I appreciate you reaching out to me. Most people that write to me think I'm a fool for going the "volunteer" route to try getting off the row. They don't understand what it feels like to have your freedom taken from you for something you didn't do. These people are trying to put an end to my life, and everybody seems to expect me to rot away in my cell for 20 or 30 years, waiting on some justice that might not never come! But I'm not about to put any faith whatsoever in this system. If the system worked, people like you and me wouldn't be in prison in the first place. I want my justice right now. Today! I'm not about to do no Nelson Mandela and then turn around and still get executed. That's torture. But I know you understand where I'm coming from. I can tell from your letter that you got that Zulu fighter mentality. Like me, you're a warrior!

I'm not go make this letter too long, but I appreciate the positive energy you directed my way. I enjoyed everything you wrote about my sister too. Whenever I get depressed, which isn't too often, I just think about her. Her memory alone gives me the strength I need to get my mind back on the right track. . . . I'm go end on that note, but stay down for your liberation, and tell Deathrow I said what's up!

Against all odds,
Mario Sanchez

Mario's letter definitely helped me shake the depression, but it didn't stop me from resenting the DWO who wouldn't let me attend my mother's funeral. I wanted to do something *real foul* to that heartless bastard like throw a cup of shit in his face if I caught him walking the range one day. But like all the other administrative clowns who ran the prison from afar, such as the Warden, the Institutional Inspector, and the Major, he rarely walked the ranges inside any cellblocks. My second Parole Board hearing was right around the corner anyhow, and it was absurd for me to be thinking about an assault on the Deputy Warden.

I might have had a few screws loose, but they weren't loose enough for me to abandon a chance at being granted a parole. Nothing was more important than my freedom.

Chapter Thirty-One

(Parole Board, second hearing: October 1999)

It's said that time flies when you're having fun. But for me in prison time always seemed to be standing still. And of all the time I served, no days were longer than that summer of 1999, when I was in AC. The ventilation system didn't work, and the humid, scorching air that soared into the 90's almost every day made it feel like I was doing time in a steam bath. But what was worse was the absence of the sights and sounds of the general population, the social atmosphere I'd grown accustomed to before they railroaded me into AC.

I couldn't meet other people at meals or recreation or library sessions or other group programs. Except for yelling over the range, I couldn't interact with anyone. Even on the five days a week when I got out of my cell for an hour of recreation, I couldn't really talk with anyone because the recreation areas had concrete partitions that kept anyone inside the 16 by 20 foot enclosure from seeing into any of the other stations. I never thought of myself as a sociable person but after months in solitary, I wanted to socialize with *anybody*.

I began to feel like a bald tire, worn down from months of isolation in the control unit, and it seemed to be breaking my mind. How my sanity survived through that summer of sweaty torture I'll never know, but I remember the relief in late September, when the cooler temperatures came, and I knew I was scheduled to go for my second Parole Board hearing.

In spite of the fierce psychological turbulence that kicked my ass the summer of 1999, I was feeling better by fall, but one thing bothered me: it was listening to a cellblock full of grown-ass-men yelling at the top of their lungs, arguing about bullshit like brushing their teeth and cleaning their cells. It made no sense for them to be bickering like a bunch of teenage girls, but they did. I felt like I was stuck in a world ruled by ignorance.

As the saying goes, ignorance is bliss—for a fool, that is.

As much as I hated the meaningless arguments, I knew if I told somebody to shut the fuck up, I'd be verbally counter-attacked by nearly everybody in the block. In addition to being severely outnumbered by the flock of fools—and all of them would have been glad to throw some feces—I knew if they teamed up against me, they would team up against Deathrow too because the two of us were cool. I didn't want him to get caught up in any mayhem so I kept my mouth shut, and I put my focus on my next Parole Board hearing.

It felt like forever since my first Parole Board hearing three years earlier, and I wasn't optimistic because I was going before them while I was in AC. At the same time, I felt a *small* bit of happiness about the pivotal day for the simple reason that I'd made it through three years of adversity without losing my mind.

I went before the Parole Board for the second time early in the morning, and I was feeling kind of sluggish. My hands were cuffed behind my back, and the leg irons seemed shorter than usual as an officer escorted me to the same run-down conference room where I'd gone before. I expected to see the same preppy, Black hearing officer who flopped me like a flapjack three years earlier, and it took me a while to figure out *nobody* was going to be in the room with me. The whole thing was going to be conducted on closed-circuit, video-conferencing television. A large TV monitor with a video camera attached to its top was mounted on the wall in front of my chair. It was on, and it displayed a live image of an empty chair and desk. After about five minutes an attractive brown-skin woman in a tan business suit came into the frame with a thick file folder. She put the folder on the desk, took a seat, and said, "Good morning, Mr. Jordan. How are you doing today, sir?"

I smiled even though I was nervous. "I'm doing okay, considering the circumstances. But I'd be doing better if I was free."

She smiled back. "I bet you would, Mr. Jordan, and in a moment we're going to see how close we can come to making that happen. But let me introduce myself. I'm Sonia Gates. I'm a senior hearing officer here in Columbus with the Adult Parole Authority. I've been on the Parole Board for more than ten years, and I've presided over hundreds of parole hearings. That said, Mr. Jordan, I'll begin by saying I've reviewed your entire file, and I don't understand why you were given 36 months at your first hearing. I can't find any aggravated factors, and I see your co-defendant was paroled last year."

"Wait a minute, Ms Gates," I interrupted. "You mean to tell me my co-defendant is already out of prison?"

"He was paroled out of state in April of last year."

"Out of state? Out of state where?"

Ms. Gates put both arms out in front of her well-endowed upper body with her palms facing me as though she was some kind of traffic cop signaling me to stop. "Calm down, Mr. Jordan, calm down," she said, smiling again. "You're upset, but don't mess this up. I'm in your corner on this one. Do yourself a favor and take a deep breath."

I tried it. I took a deep breath. "I didn't mean to raise my voice Ms Gates. I apologize."

"You're okay, and you don't owe me any apologies. But you need to tell me why you're in Administrative Control. Are you planning to be a professional boxer when you get out? I'm just asking because you must be a real dangerous fighter if they put you in Administrative Control for throwing a punch."

I relaxed a little with her light-hearted question. "Not trying to be no boxer, Ms. Gates," I said, staring straight into the lens of the video camera. "And I'm not dangerous. . . . I'm go fight to defend myself in this predatory environment, but I don't pose a threat to anybody. The so-called fight that put me in AC wasn't a real fight. I didn't throw one punch, plus—I'm embarrassed to tell you this—I *got knocked out*. Completely out. Fast asleep. There's no way I should *ever* been put in AC, Ms. Gates. No way."

Ms. Gates looked like she was taking a deep breath. "Well," she said, "guess what?"

"What?"

"Not only should you not have been placed in Administrative Control, but you probably shouldn't be in prison right now. I take pride in doing my job, and I don't give inmates continuances just to be giving them continuances. I pay *close* attention to the record when it comes to making parole decisions. Your disciplinary record is nearly flawless, and it sounds like you got placed in AC for being assaulted. I didn't have to read far in your file to get the feeling you were railroaded. But I wanted to hear you tell me about the incident carefully in your own words just in case I missed something. Now I'm sure I didn't. So taking that into account, along with the fact that you've already served beyond the time you would have had to serve if you'd been convicted under the new law, I don't see why you shouldn't be granted a parole. *Today!*"

Her words made me worry at first that I might be dreaming. Then they triggered an explosion of endorphins. "*Today*!" I said excitedly, "You mean to tell me I'm not getting flopped today?"

Ms. Gates smiled, and I'm pretty sure she winked. "I told you I was on your side on this one. And don't think it's because of those pretty brown eyes either, young man. *You did your time*—that's why I'm on your side. Five minutes into reading your file I was pretty sure I'd be on your side."

Now I was trying not to smile too much, especially about my eyes. But it had been a long time since I'd talked with a woman who didn't look like a sumo wrestler, and I couldn't stop myself. Ms. Gates was beautiful! And she had more to say. "See," she said, pausing, "unlike some of my colleagues, I give inmates their due, no matter what they've been locked up for. A few of my colleagues think justice is served by keeping offenders locked up as long as they can. But that isn't justice, and it certainly isn't rehabilitation. What it is, I say, is an abuse of power. I don't abuse my authority, Mr. Jordan—never have, never will. When somebody comes before me, and they qualify for parole according to the criteria set forth in the Ohio Revised Code, it's my duty to grant them their freedom, and that's why I'm paroling you."

For many days and many long nights it seemed as if this liberating moment would never arrive. Now that it had, the sudden reality of the end of six long nightmare years of bondage made everything seem surreal. Jimi Hendrix, *sober and drug-free surreal!*

I felt like the happiest person in prison. But when I got back to my cell and broke the news to my neighbor Deathrow, I quickly realized he was happier for me than I was. "Hallelujah! Hal-le-lujah!" he shouted when he saw my faxed Parole Board Decision Sheet. "They let my nephew go, y'all! They let the boy go!"

I knew Deathrow was going to be excited about my news, but I didn't expect him to start shouting the gospel like T.D. Jakes in a Sunday morning service. I didn't have anybody in my circle that I considered a friend except for Deathrow, and it made me feel great to see him in the highest of spirits in his ripe old age.

Deathrow and I got to be friends during the first few months we were in AC, and over time our friendship grew into something as close-knit and strong as a family bond, and somewhere along the way we started calling each other *uncle* and *nephew*. Maybe the reason we bonded like that was I hadn't ever had a real father, and he didn't have any children. Somewhere, deep down, there were voids in both of us that made our friendship important. I can't be sure about the reasons for this bonding. We never talked about why we clicked the way we did. It just wasn't the kind of thing serious convicts talked about.

When I first went into prison and was a rookie at doing time, I paid close attention to the talk of other inmates. One thing I noticed right away was something phony about most prison friendships. Instead of dudes keeping things real, just being cool with each other in authentic ways, they put on acts, pretending they were friends so they could get something—money, food, sex, drugs, maybe protection. I soon realized I was in an unprincipled, survival-of-the-fittest environment. A day didn't go by in AC without somebody gossiping over the range, berating and belittling or scheming on somebody they were supposed to be cool with. Not me and Deathrow though. We didn't partake in any of that soft shit. We minded our own business. We never talked down on one another, and we never allowed anybody to manipulate us against each other, which a lot of our miserable peers seemed to enjoy doing to people just for the sake of doing it.

As solid as the bond between Deathrow and me was, I did notice a small crack. Deathrow wouldn't tell me why he was in AC. I asked him more than once, and all he would say was he'd gotten caught up in a Catch-22. Finally, I let it go, but in the back of the mind I wanted to know what he done. Telling me he was in AC because of a Catch-22 was too vague to cut it for me. He seemed to be hiding something. But I let it go, figuring he was entitled to keep it to himself. Plus, I had a great deal of admiration for the man, being that he had fought his way off death row. I wasn't about to be pestering him with the same question over and over again. And even though I didn't know why Deathrow was in AC, I knew for a fact I was going to miss the old man when I got out of prison.

But I was anxious as hell to get released. Normally, it took about 30 days for all the paperwork to get processed, but I didn't have any addresses of family or friends listed on my Parole Release Form—places I could be paroled to. So I had to be paroled to a halfway house, which was a much longer process. They told me 60 to 90 days.

It was 65 days since I met with the Parole Board when my patience started running thin. Christmas was about two weeks away, and I desperately wanted to get out before all the holiday hoopla cranked up. If I didn't, I would almost certainly be waiting another month, and at this stage of my incarceration, a month felt like a year. I was weary of waiting for mail call and the notice of my release, and I felt like it was never going to come. Then, on December 10, 1999, I got my notice. "Please be advised, Mr. Jordan," it began, "that on December 13, 1999, you will be discharged from the Cumberland Correctional Institution and transferred to the New Life transitional housing facility located in Cleveland, Ohio."

The nightmare was finally over.

I spent most of my last weekend in prison thinking about the things I'd have to take care of as soon as I got out: getting a state I.D. card, applying for emergency welfare assistance, and—most importantly—filling out job applications. I had some ideas about taking care of everything, courtesy of the time I spent in the independent living program at The Empowerment after I got kicked out George Junior Republic. It was a while back, but I remembered. Despite those insights though, the shift from prison to society looked difficult as I sat in my cell.

My main support in the years before I went to prison was my poor, drug-addicted mother. It wasn't the greatest, but it was support, and now I didn't have any from anybody on the outside. I was going to be homeless, a thought that made me very nervous.

After six years in prison, I should have had "specific steps and approaches" for getting on my feet and earning an honest living. But I'd been a procrastinating dumb-ass, and I didn't have even the beginning of a plan. Early in my incarceration, when I had more motivation, I spent some time thinking about starting a business and a summer basketball league for at-risk youth. But thinking was as far as I got with those ideas. I spent too much time daydreaming about miraculously getting out of prison and making it big by playing basketball. I should have been learning something new for my future. I had a burning passion for that basketball dream back then, and I don't regret my efforts to make it work. But I do regret that I didn't recognize when it was time to let the dream go.

As my release date careened toward me, I tried to pull a rabbit out of a hat and come up with a quick entrepreneurial plan that I could put down once I got out. I tried from the Saturday evening of my last weekend until I fell asleep, and when I woke up, I kept trying, but I couldn't think of anything. Finally, I gave up and started thinking of Mario, my homeboy. I hadn't heard from him since the beginning of the year, when he wrote me the first time. I wanted to write and see how he was doing, plus tell him I'd gotten paid at the Parole Board, but he hadn't answered my last letter, and I didn't want to bother him with letters that were essentially trivial *when he was less than six months away, possibly, from being executed.*

An article I'd read in the *Columbus Dispatch* a few months earlier said Mario's execution date was going to be set for somewhere between the end of spring and the middle of next year, 2000. The former date was just around the corner, and being that I hadn't heard or read about any new developments with his case, I had to assume his "volunteering" wasn't unfolding the way he'd imagined it would. And if it wasn't working out, then it made sense why Mario hadn't been staying in contact. The man was preoccupied with the fight of his life *for his life*.

If I was on death row for a crime I didn't commit, and I was five or six months from being executed, I probably wouldn't be writing many letters to somebody I'd just met in prison.

I sprawled out on my bed thinking from the time I woke in the morning until almost dinnertime, when I heard Deathrow pounding on my wall.

"What's up wit ya old man?" I shouted, sort of smiling to myself.

"Man, you know what's up. You ain't said two words to me all day! Did ya think you was go sleep your last day off like that?"

I pushed my blankets off me and sat up in bed. "Naw, it ain't like that. I just been over here doing some serious thinking, that's all."

"You over there worrying about something. I can tell."

I slid down to the end of my bed, towards the front of my cell. "You right, I was worrying a little bit this morning and last night. But it wasn't anything too serious. Just trying to brainstorm up on a plan to make some money, honestly. When you knocked on the wall, I wasn't even thinking about any of that. I was wondering what's up with Mario and his case. Still ain't heard back from him, you know."

"Well, it ain't nothing you can do right now about either one of those situations. So don't stress yourself out, nephew. You'll be alright once you get to that halfway house. They got programs there to help you out, get your career going. You go have to be patient. I know I told you a thousand times, but believe me, you got. . .to. . .be. . .patient. Hey, speaking of Mario, I used to tell him the same thing when we was on the row together. He'd be asking me about how to file a motion on his case, and I'd tell him just a little—I didn't know that much my damn self—and the next thing I know he'd go and file a motion about something he didn't know nothing about. And now he went and did that volunteering to be executed mess, and it ain't no taking that back. I know his reasons for going that route, but I believe the boy should have let the system run its course instead of getting all impatient and doing what he did. But, hey, what's done is done. I'm just trying to offer you a few pearls of wisdom on your way out the door."

Me and Deathrow stayed up to the wee hours talking and laughing like two kids in a tree house on a summer sleep-over. I don't know when I fell asleep, but I dozed off on

Deathrow when he was talking to me about something. The last thing I remember him saying is something about Tupac. It ain't no telling just what he was talking about because that man could talk for hours about anything.

I wish I could have known Deathrow back when I was a fatherless, misguided adolescent. If I'd known him then, I'm almost certain I would never have come to prison. If there weren't so many Black men like Deathrow sitting in prison, the ravished and impoverished Black communities all over the U.S. might be thriving instead of producing generations of career criminals. I wished Deathrow could be getting out with me.

But barring death or escape, *he never was getting out.*

Chapter Thirty-Two

"Keep ya head up out there, nephew!" Deathrow shouted as I walked down the stairs off my range. I was uncuffed and carrying a yellow net bag with my property in it, on my way to Receiving and Delivery, where I could get processed and released. "And don't come back!" he added.

I stopped at the bottom of the stairs when I heard Deathrow. "You ain't never *never* go see me again in this bitch, Unc," I shouted. "I'm going out there to *live*!"

My "free at last" moment came in the morning around 10:30. Much to my surprise, it only took about an hour for the same fat, lightning bolt tattooed officer who processed me into CCI to process me out. He took a couple of mug shots of me and had me change into a pair of tan pants and a tan shirt. He gave me a tan jacket with a white envelope sticking out of a pocket. I knew it held the $70 gate money. After I sat on a beat-up old wooden bench for ten minutes, a tall, clean-shaven Black guy in mirror-tint aviator sunglasses and a dark blue snowsuit with "New Life" embroidered on the front came around the corner. "You ready to get the hell out of here, my man?" he asked in a raspy voice without looking at me.

I stared at him like he was crazy until he looked my way. "Hell yeah," I said, grinning. "I been ready."

I didn't know the halfway house was picking me up. I thought I'd be riding a bus back home by myself, and I didn't think I'd be supervised by anybody until I got to the halfway house. But despite the perversion of my first taste of freedom, my walk across the snow-covered prison parking lot to the New Life transport van had an amazing feeling of freedom.

No more handcuffs. No more strip searches. No more empty mail calls. Just freedom.

The whole state of Ohio was blanketed with snow on the morning I was released, and driving conditions were horrendous. Normally, it takes about five hours from

Portsmouth to Cleveland, but the New Life guy figured our trip was more likely to take eight. He stopped at a BP station a few minutes outside the prison and had me pick out some snacks for the trip, at his expense. I'd had my mind kind of set on Burger King, but I didn't waste any time worrying about that. I went right to work picking out some junk food. I grabbed some candy bars, bags of Ruffles potato chips, some chocolate milk, and maybe ten packages of honey-roasted peanuts. By the time we got to Columbus, about three and a half hours later, I had a terrible stomachache.

Clutching my stomach, I dozed off, listening to an unfamiliar song on the radio, and when I woke, it was dark. We were riding through downtown Cleveland. I put my hands on top of my head and whispered to myself, "I made it!"

I felt like a tourist in my own city, taking in the holiday atmosphere, trying to see everything. The city was decorated with thousands of lights, and even though I hadn't really felt the holiday for a long time, I was in awe of how beautiful and lively the city looked. I saw parents walking with their kids and beautiful women of all hues walking and talking on their cell phones. Plus, I seen two horse-drawn carriages trotting up Euclid Avenue as we rode through historic Public Square.

Being back in Cleveland, my city, the home of gorgeous, super-sexy Halle Berry—it felt terrific. I felt like maybe I could cross her path somehow and make her mine. But so did all of her other millions of admirers.

Sweeping Halle Berry off her feet was going to have to wait though. I had greater challenges rooted in reality: getting *on my feet* and making it out of the halfway house.

The New Life house, on West 25th Street on Cleveland's west side, was an old red brick two-story building. It was ten minutes from downtown in a decent neighborhood of mainly White, blue-collar residents. I was shocked by how normal it looked because I was expecting something with fences and barbed wire. It looked like an ordinary old apartment building.

The New Life driver, whose name I never did get, parked on the curb in front of the house and walked me up an unshoveled walkway to the front door. He pushed the intercom button, and pretty soon an older man's voice came on, crackling. "Who goes there?" He sounded like a pirate in a Disney film.

The driver leaned in toward the intercom. "This transpo wit' ya new arrival. Open on up, it's freezing out here!"

The old pirate buzzed us inside to a narrow hallway that led to a door secured by two dead bolts that he unlocked and let us in. "Man, I been waiting on y'all for more than three hours." He was a tall, slender bearded man who looked a lot younger than he sounded. "I thought y'all got your asses in a wreck."

The driver smiled. "Come on, Stu, you *know* I drive too good for that. Them damn roads, man, they was terrible!"

"Well," Stu said, stepping out of the doorway, "are y'all go come inside or just stand there?"

The driver handed Stu a thick manila folder. "That's all his paperwork they gave me," he said. "I got to get down to the garage and pick up my truck so I'm about to go ahead and get on out of here, Stu. You still got to take your newbie through orientation anyhow."

As soon as the driver left, Stu the pirate man had me follow him through the empty, well-lit living room area into the dining room, where he told me to take a chair next to him at the large, oak table. "Before I get all the way started," he said, "I just want to tell you I call everybody here by their last names to avoid any mix-ups. Couple of years ago I had four guys in here named Mike, and I got 'em all mixed up *everyday*. One of 'em got happy feet one day and went AWOL on me, and when I notified my supervisor and called the police, I gave the wrong damn name. They ended up arresting the wrong guy at his job *on his first week there*.

Both of us erupted in laughter.

"Hey," I said, as I wiped away tears from laughing so hard, "you don't got nobody else in here named Malcolm Jordan, do you?"

"You the only youngsta in here with that name. I'm certain of that. And speaking of names, I go by Stu or Mr. Preston. Some of the guys think I'm an old man, I guess, because of my voice. So they call me Mr. Preston. But it only sound this way because I had throat cancer before. I'm still in my forties, shit." Stu paused and checked the time on his calculator watch. "Enough about me, though, Jordan. I got to get these rules and regulations run down to you before everybody gets back for curfew."

"What time is curfew?"

"Sunday through Thursday it's 9:30. Friday and Saturday it's 11. But if you get a job on the graveyard shift, you're exempt from curfew. You go be on probation for 30 days, Jordan, so you're not go be able to go out in the evening. All your passes are 10 a.m. to 4 p.m. And anytime you leave out of the building—*and I mean anytime*—you have to log it in the itinerary book. You have to document what time you leave, where you're going, and when you'll be back. This is important, Jordan. Always remember to sign that book. As for rules inside the building. . .no drugs or alcohol, which I'm sure you know already." I nodded. "No weapons, which you probably know too. No smoking on the premises. No cooking in the microwave past 10 p.m. unless you work the graveyard shift. No loud music whatsoever. Only person gets to play loud music is me when I play my Stevie Wonder, once in a blue moon. Some of the other staff are more lenient and will let you blast the stereo. But on my—"

"How many staff work here with you?" I interrupted.

"Altogether, it's just four of us. Two regulars work Mondays through Thursdays, and two reliefs work Fridays through Sundays. "I'm the afternoon regular, and a Black guy named Mr. Enis is the other regular. He works from midnight to noon. He'll be here when you wake up tomorrow. He's an older guy, late fifties, and he's been working here for close to twenty years. He'll help you with whatever you need. So in the morning if you have questions—and you will, trust me—just ask him. He'll get you together. As far as the relief staff, in the afternoons a short Black woman, Karen Elliot, will be here. I don't know her that well. She's only been here for a few months, but the residents tell me she's cool. And from midnight to noon the relief staff is a cool cat named Mitchell Thomas, a guy I went to college with down at Tri-C. He used to work with me at the big Harbor Lights halfway house over on the east side."

"That's where I'm from," I said quickly, "the east side. Why didn't they send me over there?"

Stu frowned and shook his head. "You don't want to be in that place, young brotha. That spot is, like, the damn projects. It's loud as hell, dirty, and they got over 200 people in that place! Where you're at right now is about as good as it gets in a halfway house around here. We got twelve people in here. Plus you got your own room. But believe me when I tell you," Stu's voice dropped to a raspy whisper, "if you screw up here, that's where they go put you! You got to keep your nose *clean* to stay in here."

Suddenly a question I'd meant to ask popped up in my head. "Speaking of keeping my nose clean," I asked, "how often do I have to take drug tests in here?"

"We don't have any specific schedule. We do random tests. Your parole officer, a White guy named Mr. Schubert, is the person who administers the urinalysis test. You'll meet him tomorrow, and now that I think about it, he'll probably take you to get some clothes too if the weather ain't that bad."

"Y'all buy all our clothes for us?" I asked, trying not to sound surprised.

Stu flashed a grin. "In your dreams, mister. This ain't no Wells Fargo. We give ya'll a $300 clothes voucher when you first get here, and after that you're on your own."

"So what about, like, soap and toothpaste and stuff?"

"You don't have to worry about any of that. It's a big plastic bag upstairs on your bed with enough cosmetics to last you a month. There's some packages of socks and underwear in there too. Plus, if you want a haircut, we got a resident that's a pretty decent barber, name of Polk. He's a tall Black dude about your height. He'll be here in the morning so just talk to him, and he'll get you together."

When Stu finished my orientation, I headed for my bedroom and called it a night before the other residents got back for curfew. I was drowsy, plus I wanted to sit in the cut and listen to my surroundings. I wanted a better feel for the kind of environment I'd be living in.

My bedroom wasn't much bigger than my cell. But it was way more comfortable and cleaner. It smelled like it had been cleaned top to bottom with some kind of orange-scented disinfectant. It had a soft twin-size bed with a down-filled, maroon comforter. The walls were sky blue and graffiti-free. At the foot of my bed, next to my small, wood dresser that doubled as a desk, there was a big venetian-blind-covered window that overlooked West 25th Street.

To somebody who hadn't been incarcerated, my room might have looked bad. But it felt wonderful! The only semblance of a complaint I could have imagined was that I didn't have a TV set or radio in my room. I had gotten so excited when I learned about the parole that I signed a "property waiver" and donated my TV to a random inmate in need of one. But the room was terrific.

After lying in bed for an hour listening to people get back for curfew, I was exhausted. I closed my eyes and pulled my comforter snugly up over my head. For the first time in years, my mind and body felt totally relaxed. I felt at peace. I slept like a baby.

The next morning, after an early shower, I met Mr. Enis and a few of the other residents during breakfast. They all were Black, and they looked to be in their thirties except, of course, Mr. Enis, who was going bald. Normally, the staff just cooked lunch and dinner, but Mr. Enis fixed pancakes and sausages on my first morning at the New Life house. He said I deserved a big breakfast after being in prison for so long. I agreed, and I did what he wanted, eating eight pancakes and maybe a dozen sausage links before I got up from the table.

After breakfast I watched TV in the living room and waited on the barber, Polk, to come downstairs so I could ask for a haircut. When he came downstairs, though, I didn't know it was him until I heard Mr. Enis use his name when he asked him how many pancakes he could eat. After he finished eating, I asked him about a haircut, and he nodded and went back upstairs to get his clippers. Once he got me on a chair in the laundry room, it took him less than twenty minutes, and he did a superb job too.

"Damn, my nigga," I said to Polk, who was just a little over two years older than me at 27. I was looking in the mirror he handed me. "This is a perfect fade. You should be working at a barber shop."

Polk smiled. "That's what everybody tell me, man. I'm thinking about going to get my license. I want to open up my own shop one day, to be honest with you. But right now I just work my little Taco Bell gig, stack some bread, *and get the fuck out this bitch*!"

"This spot ain't messed up like that is it?" I asked.

"Oh, naw, it ain't bad here. I'm just trying to get out of here so I can get custody of my son, man. I been missing in his life off-and-on for the last six years, and he just turned eight-years-old in October. Already his bad ass been suspended from school for punching a little girl in the face." Polk paused and shook his head. "I ain't about to let my son get caught up in this jail bullshit though. His mama can't handle him, and she want me to raise him anyhow. So I'm just trying to get my shit together, man."

"Why not just move in with your son's mother?"

Polk let out a quick sigh and smiled. "Man," he said loudly, "that'll *never* happen. That crazy bitch don't know how to keep other nigga's dicks out her mouth—*or her pussy.*"

I slapped my hands on the side of my head and leaned back in my chair, trying to hold in my laughter, but I couldn't. "Polk, man," I hesitated, "you's a silly guy, my nigga. How you go just cap on the mother of your son like that? She the mama bear, man."

"I know who she is. But, hey, it is what it is with her. She's a slut, and that's just the way it is."

I smiled and shrugged. "Well, since you putting it like that, do she got any single sisters you can hook me up with?"

Polk started laughing and wagged his index finger at me. "Ohhh," he said, slowly, "I see what's up now. You ready to get you some pussy, huh?" I laughed and started to speak, but he kept on talking. "Ain't nothing wrong with that, man. If I did all them years, I'd probably go AWOL to get me some. My son's mama don't got no sisters, but next time I call her, I'm go see if she'll give me her cousin Carol's phone number for you. You can call her and shoot your shot. These phones in here are just like the ones in the joint though. So until you can leave on a day pass, you have to call her collect. They should be letting you leave in the next few days so you'll be cool in a minute. But Carol, my nigga—man, she look *good as hell.*"

"What she look like?" I asked, trying to sound cool.

"Aw, man—she about five-six, brown-skinned, light brown eyes, real petite. She probably weigh about a hundred pounds, but she built like that girl Jasmine Guy that played on that one show back in the day."

I started thinking about Carol, wondering what her voice sounded like. What kind of hairstyle did she wear? Later that morning, as I was lying in my bed waiting for my PO, Mr. Schubert, to arrive, I kept thinking about Carol, and my thoughts turned lustful, pornographic. I'd been deprived of the companionship of a woman since I was arrested, in 1993, and the possibility that I might be within a stone's throw of getting close to a woman pushed my hormones into overdrive. One thing led to another, and ten minutes after I laid down, I caved in and started masturbating so vigorously that right after I blew my load, my horny ass fell asleep, lying on my back *with my pants and underwear draped around my ankles.* I don't know how long I was sleeping like that, but I woke up in the nick of time, just before Mr. Enis and my PO came barging into my room.

While I was sleeping in my self-induced, post-masturbation state, my PO arrived at the house. He asked Mr. Enis to get me, and when Mr. Enis called my name a few times without getting an answer, they thought I might have gotten a case of "happy feet." So they ran their Mel Gibson and Danny Glover asses up to my bedroom to see if I was still on the set. When they seen I hadn't taken the Underground Railroad, my PO introduced himself and asked why I didn't respond.

"I was asleep, Mr. Schubert," I said. "I ain't hear *nothing.*"

Mr. Schubert was six-four and muscular and looked to be in his late forties. He gave my room a quick once-over before he spoke. "Well, I think you go have to wash your ears out and make sure you get a good night's rest. Now grab your jacket over there so we can get out of here."

After nearly getting caught in my most embarrassing moment, I felt mainly relieved after I tidied myself up in the bathroom and grabbed my jacket.

My PO drove a 4 by 4 Ford F150, and he was in a rush to get me out to buy some clothes before the weather turned bad. My first impression was that Mr. Schubert was an asshole, but by the time he'd taken me to get a state ID and a 30-day RTA bus pass, I was beginning to change my mind. Then he treated me to an all-you-can-eat McDonald's lunch, and I was pretty sure I'd had him wrong. It took me a half hour, but I put down two Big Macs, a large order of fries, two pieces of apple pie, and a medium strawberry shake. Then Mr. Schubert drove me downtown to Custer's, an army surplus store where everybody with clothes vouchers shopped.

Custer's had bargains but not many brands to choose from. They had mostly no-name brands, but that didn't bother me, and I bought myself some sets of brown, black, and dark blue work pants and shirts, two hooded sweat shirts, two skullcaps, and a heavy black winter coat. I splurged on a pair of Timberland boots. Those were must-haves during the cold winters in Cleveland.

After buying the clothes, I wrapped up my day with my PO by picking up some job applications from fast-food restaurants along the same strip with Custer's. I filled out the applications, and Mr. Schubert said he'd turn them in the next day.

All I could do now was be patient with life and stay consistent with doing it.

My first day pass came through two days after that, and I headed for a nearby library. While I was in prison, I heard lots of talk about the amazing Internet, and I had to see if for myself.

On my way to the library I stopped at a pay phone to call Carol. I'd spoken to her the day before, after Polk gave me her number, but this time I couldn't get through. We'd talked for an hour during that first conversation, and I was hoping to make some arrangements *so we could meet in person.* She had told me she was 27 years old and didn't have any children, and she had her own apartment in a decent neighborhood. She didn't have a car, but she did have a job as a manager at KFC. I think I was in love before I hung up the phone.

The library was virtually empty, and the librarian, a fat, older Black lady, started me on a computer. She showed me some basics, and in less than half an hour I was navigating my way through the World Wide Web like Bill Gates.

The first site I logged onto, once I got the hang of it, was the Ohio Department of Rehabilitation and Corrections. I wanted to find out where my sleazy co-defendant got paroled to. It turned out the maggot was in Gary, Indiana. When I seen on the computer screen that he was living in a neighboring state, I thought for a few seconds of paying his lying ass a visit, once I got off parole, and putting him in a full body cast. But any kind of serious violence laid on him would most likely lead right back to me so I stopped thinking about it.

I lost track of time on the Internet and ended up rushing out of the library and back to the halfway house barely in time for my early curfew. On my way back I realized I'd forgotten to look up the status of Mario's death penalty case so the next day I went back to the library and logged onto an anti-death penalty site. In their Current News section I found a headline:

Execution Date Set in Controversial Case
Sanchez Slated to Die June of 2000 in Ohio

After living through years of injustice in Ohio's criminal justice system, I wasn't really surprised about Mario. But I'd been hoping for the best even though I knew he was on death row in a state that loved executions. Now I knew for sure the state was *psychologically torturing him.*

Chapter Thirty-Three

It took me roughly two weeks of talking on pay phones inside freezing cold phone booths before Carol agreed to let me meet her at her apartment. I had thought she would invite me sooner, but she told me she was a patient type and she wanted to check me out before she gave me her address. As eager as I was to meet her, I respected her for making me wait. It let me know she was responsible about taking care of herself, which was something I'd learned to value in a woman. After my relationship with Sharon, my co-defendant's scandalous cousin, I wasn't hoping to meet no more hoodrats. I wanted a real woman in my life.

It was late in the morning of the day before New Year's Eve when I finally met Carol after close to an hour on the bus. She lived in a one-bedroom apartment in a row-house style complex on the east side of the city close to Warrensville Heights. I took a nervous deep breath and rang her doorbell, and after a few moments she came to the door.

"And who might you be?" she asked in a soft tone of voice, leaving the door chain up.

"Malcolm," I said, grinning. "Malcolm, the pay phone man."

She laughed and unchained the door. "I knew it was you, silly," she said through the screen door as she unlatched it and pulled it open so I could see her for the first time.

Between talking with her on the phone and listening to Polk's description, I expected her to be easy on the eyes. But she was beautiful! She was wearing skintight jeans and a small gray tee shirt, shoeless, with a pair of little black footies on. I lost my train of thought just looking at her.

She flashed a smile and rescued me from making a fool of myself. "Are you go come in before all my heat gets out?" she asked as she stepped to the side. "I'm not trying to heat up the whole neighborhood, Malcolm the pay phone man."

I snapped out of my trance and walked inside the warm, carpeted apartment, and I was laughing at myself as I took off my coat and boots by the door. She had me sit down on the living room couch while she fixed us giant mugs of hot chocolate, and then she sat down beside me, and we talked. I was trying hard to listen more than talk, but Carol, who was born Caroline Theresa Austin, kept telling me to keep talking. I'd told her about George Junior Republic, my mother's battle with drugs, my love of basketball, my time in prison, and she still wanted to hear more. I found it flattering after six years without a woman showing any interest in me, but I wanted to know about her.

"I been talking about me long enough," I said to Carol as I pointed my finger at her. "It's your turn now."

She smiled and seemed surprised that I wanted to know her story. "My story is *boring*," she said. "You don't want to hear about my uneventful life."

I grinned and shook my head. "I don't know what you talking about. I'd sit here and listen to you say your ABC's."

Carol burst out laughing. "ABC's huh? Seriously, Malcolm, the reason I ain't tell you too much about me already on the phone, it's because I thought you might be trying to run a little game on me so you could try and get you some. I wasn't about to, just, open up to you, *not like that*."

"So," I smiled and hesitated, "so all this time you been thinking I was lying to you?"

She sucked her teeth and puckered her lips at me and grinned. "You know what I'm talking about, boy. Don't make me jump across this couch and beat up on you. I might have to mess up that handsome face of yours."

I smiled at her compliment. "So you think I'm handsome, huh?"

Carol ran her hand over her permed, shoulder-length hair. "Yeah," she smiled, "you definitely decent. You could use a little Ambi face soap, though, to even out your complexion."

I rubbed my cheek. "You right about that for sure. But you sure don't need any Ambi."

"Why you say that?" she asked, opening her beautiful brown eyes real wide like she didn't know the answer.

"Because you look *almost* as good as Halle Berry."

She laughed and leaned over to punch me on my leg. "That ain't funny," she said. "I look *better* than Halle Berry, for your information!"

"Alright then, can I ask you one question, Ms. Better-than-Halle-Berry?"

"What you wanna know?"

I hesitated, took a sip of hot chocolate. "What I want to know—and I'm serious, too—is how in the world does somebody as fine as you *not* have a boyfriend?"

She smiled. "You sure do know how to sneak in a compliment. . . . Okay, seriously, I don't have a boyfriend because all those wannabes out here, they *ain't about shit*."

She sounded real serious. "Why you say that?" I asked.

Carol let out a sigh. "Why I say that is because all these niggas want to do is sell crack, shoot people, disrespect their women, and not take care of their kids. And it ain't no way in hell I'm going to tolerate any of that. *Hell* no! And after everything I already told you I went through with my last boyfriend, it really ain't no way."

My head was nodding before my mind was thinking she was right, and I was quiet for a while. Finally, I asked, "Okay then, what makes me so special? *I'm an ex-con!*"

She took a while to answer. "Malcolm, you talk about stuff I ain't never heard nobody talk about except my grandfather, before he passed."

"What kind of stuff you mean?"

"You know, the stuff about *self-empowerment* that you be talking about. Don't nobody out here talk positive like that. I mean you just seem *different*. Even though I said I thought you might just be on the prowl, just trying to get you some, if I didn't think you had some good qualities about yourself, trust me, you wouldn't be sitting on my couch right now."

Once I got Carol talking, she really opened up. She talked, practically uninterrupted, for the last hour I was at her apartment, and my intuition told me she'd been wanting to talk to somebody who listened and really paid attention for a long time. She told me about her immediate family, from whom she'd been estranged for over a year. Her father, a retired steelworker, had to pull a pistol on her abusive boyfriend to get him to stop beating her up every time he got drunk. After that particular incident, she said, her mother and father, both devout Christians, gave her an ultimatum: end the relationship with her abusive boyfriend, a 24 year old, unemployed pretty boy, or move out. Carol, an only child, was fed up with her parents' constant nagging so she decided to move out *and* kick her boyfriend to the curb. She moved into the apartment and established her independence for the first time, but she said she sometimes regretted moving out. For one thing, it was hard financially. She was living from paycheck to paycheck, but her goal was to go back to college and finish working on a degree in Business Administration. I found that impressive because I didn't know many people who were graduating from high school, let alone college.

Listening to her, I realized Carol deserved to have an upstanding man in her life, and if she wanted to give me the chance to help her on her journey, I was ready to go along.

When it came time for me to head back to the halfway house, I didn't want to leave. But we both knew I had to get back there on time so I stood up and put on my boots and my coat. As I opened the door, Carol was standing so close by me that I could feel the warmth of her breath on my neck, and she lightly tapped me on the shoulder. "We just met, but ain't you go give me a hug?"

She caught me by surprise, again. I figured nothing like that was go happen for a while if it happened at all. But I didn't waste any time wrapping my long arms around her torso and holding her close to me. I could barely remember the last time I'd held a fine woman in my arms, but holding Carol quickly refreshed my memory. When I began to get aroused, I had to ease my body away from hers to avoid getting an embarrassing erection. The warmth and softness of her body and the light scent of the perfume on the nape of her neck were too much for my hormones to handle.

"You give good hugs," she said breathlessly as we moved apart.

I adjusted my skullcap and grinned. "Why you say that?"

She smiled. "You know why."

I shook my head and laughed. "No I don't. You gotta tell me."

Carol cut her eyes away from mine and looked down at my groin area. "That right there," she said, still sounding kind of breathless. "You know what I'm talking about too. And don't act like you don't or I'm go have to"—she playfully punched my chest—"beat you up. But I ain't mad at you, Malcolm Xavier. It's been a long time since I had me some too. *A long time!*"

When Carol admitted she knew she'd gotten me aroused and was laid back about it, I figured she wanted to have sex as much as I did, and it gave me a big boost of confidence. As I pushed open the screen door, I said, "Well, all you got to do is give me the word"—I cut my eyes down her body—"and I'll hit the button on that stopwatch whenever you want."

Carol dropped her jaw, pretending to be shocked or surprised. "Boy, you better get outta here before you miss your bus. And you better call me too tomorrow before I go to work."

Walking to the bus stop, I felt so alive I could have jogged back to the halfway house if I had time.

I ushered in the new millennium by working hard to get myself acclimated to life outside the prison. That first week of the year 2000 I was getting on and off buses, turning in job applications, and when I wasn't job hunting, I was at the library or at Carol's apartment trying to get my first piece of post-incarceration pussy. I kept a few condoms in my pocket just in case, but Carol said we weren't doing *anything* until I took an HIV test. It made sense, and she agreed to get tested with me. She made appointments for us both to get tested at a free clinic.

The next week I spent most of my time the same way, ripping and running on the bus, and I enjoyed taking in the scenery as I rode around to the various places where I applied. But I hated standing in the cold at those bus stops.

The first place Carol and me went together was a small bank in a strip mall so I could open up a savings account with a $50 deposit. This was a couple days before our appointments at the clinic, and we strolled through the mall doing some window shopping. It made me cringe a little when I realized I couldn't afford to buy Carol a pair of shoes she liked. But we went in a photography shop and I paid for some pictures of us together in front of an air-brushed backdrop of the Great Pyramids. Carol wanted to pay, but I insisted, and I bought a few extra copies to mail to Deathrow. I hadn't written to him yet. After that we took the bus back to Carol's neighborhood and shared a cheese pizza and a basket of garlic breadsticks at a pizzeria near her apartment. I walked her home and held her hand the entire way.

Carol was smiling while we walked, and when we got back to her apartment, she said nobody had ever held her hand and walked her home. I found that hard to believe, considering her looks. But I'd heard lots of stories on TV of beautiful women who were lonely, and I guess she was just one of them. When I left that day, she gave me the finest hug I ever had.

Every time I left Carol's apartment she gave me a hug, and every time she gave me a hug, my hands just started moving all over her body, trying to go inside her clothes. She stopped me every time, but I wasn't mad. I knew she was just playing an old-fashioned game of "chase the cat" with me. But on the day I walked her home, when my hands started roaming as we said goodbye, she took my hands and put them on the cuff of her ass cheeks, and when she did that, I palmed her firm buttocks and pulled her close against me. Almost instantly, my magic stick inflated like a balloon hooked up to a compressor, stiffening like a lead pipe. When she felt it pressing against her, she reached down inside my pants and started massaging what she'd created. I tried to hold back from ejaculating, but the touch of her warm, soft hand felt so fine I exploded almost immediately. We were standing by the door, and when I came and released all my pent up sexual frustration, I was in such a weakened state of ecstasy that I stumbled and nearly made us fall. We both started laughing, and then, after tidying up, we said goodbye.

The next day on the phone, Carol called our quick meeting by the door a "sexual appetizer." Two days later we got the word from the clinic that we were both HIV negative and headed back to her apartment. She was on me before I could get the door closed, kissing me French style, and as I wrapped my arms around her and was kissing her, I back-kicked the door closed. She took my hand and led me into the bedroom, where she quickly closed the curtains, kicked off her faux fur boots, and started undressing. She took off her coat and slung it on the floor. Then she unbuttoned her jeans and started working them off her beautiful ass and legs, which left me standing there admiring how she looked in a pair of panties.

When she got her jeans down to her knees, she looked up at me and grinned. "Are you go get undressed?" she asked, as I stood there staring at her skintight dark green panties. "Because, you know, that's the only way you go get some of this." Then, as she was pulling her panties down and I seen the frontal view of her nakedness, I snapped out of my state of wonderment and undressed as fast as I could, thinking what a beautiful sight her pussy was to see, which was better than any I'd ever seen before. I caught my first sight of her cupcake-sized breasts just before I pulled my sweatshirt over my head. She laid there on the bed waiting on me, and I thought for a second I wished her breasts were bigger, but her dark brown aureoles and nipples that looked like quarter-sized chocolate chips satisfied my lustful appetite.

I flopped my naked body on the unmade, queen-sized bed. I scooted over to Carol and started kissing her. She parted her silky smooth legs and pulled my arm across her breasts, letting me know she wanted me between her legs. Once I was there, I started kissing her again, and when I felt her soft and firm pussy pressing against my erection, I started licking her all over her nipples, which were hard as steel. She let out a deep, lustful moan and wrapped one of her legs around me and started caressing my lower back with her foot. That awakened my inner aggressive eroticism.

"Hold on for a second," I said as I rolled from between her legs and onto my back. "How about you get on top?"

Carol smiled. "Oh," she said in husky, sensual voice, "you want me to ride that for you?"

She swung her leg over my waist and started to get on top like a cowgirl. "Not like that," I said, and I twirled my index finger in a circular motion. "Turn the other way so I can do that *number* thing with you?"

Her eyes widened, and her jaw dropped. "You wanna *sixty-nine?"* she asked, and she sounded breathless and excited.

"Yeah. You said we could do whatever, right?"

I quickly learned Carol wasn't bashful in the bedroom. She spun around and put her golden brown derriere right in front of my face, and I grabbed her hips and pulled her mildly scented womanhood snugly up against my lips and plunged my tongue between her moist essence and gently licked her erect clitoris. When my tongue made contact, her entire body jolted, and she let out a moan of pure ecstasy. Then she got all the way with the program by taking over half of my throbbing erection inside her warm mouth. She did it skillfully, and it felt so good that my whole body tensed up with pleasure. I almost ejaculated right then, but some kind of way I staved off the quick climax. A few minutes later, though, Carol's sucking and licking brought me to an explosive orgasm, and as soon as that happened, she went into the bathroom and tidied up her hygiene, then came back in the bedroom and gave me a toothbrush so I could do the same.

We weren't finished. We did some good old-fashioned fucking doggy style, and then we did it in the missionary position, which was Carol's favorite. When we were finally done, we took a shower together, and then I had to rush a little to say goodbye and catch my bus back to the halfway house. As I hurried to the bus stop, I felt like a new person, now that I had somebody important in my life.

Me and Carol hadn't gotten to the point where we were comfortable with the word *love*, but judging by the passionate way we gave pleasure to each other on our first time, I thought it might not be long until we could say it.

Love—real love, that is—appeared to be on our horizon like an early morning sunrise.

Chapter Thirty-Four

Over the next six months, as the seasons changed, my relationship with Carol grew, and we found ways to spend more time together. She bought a used Jeep Grand Cherokee at the beginning of spring, and she started routinely picking me up every day at the halfway house. We went to movies, restaurants, the library, the car wash, and I even let her talk me into going to the Cleveland Art Museum. I was in love, and I figured if she wanted to go to a million art museums, I'd go. And the day we went to the museum, Carol told me she knew for sure I loved her.

A couple weeks after we went to the art museum, I decided it was time to visit my mother's burial site, and I told Carol I was go catch a bus out there to the cemetery. I didn't think she'd be comfortable going with me, being that she didn't ever know my mother. We were sitting on her couch when I told her, and she crossed her arms and just stared daggers through me. She didn't say a word. But she looked so sexy and beautiful sitting there that I just stared back, studying her face.

After a while she told me she was going with me. She was supposed to be by my side in difficult times, she said, and when I seen how emotional she was about supporting me, there wasn't any doubt in my mind: she loved me.

Two months later, a day before Mother's Day, Carol was talking to me on the phone when she suddenly asked me to move in with her. I was tempted, but I hadn't found a job. She was trying to help me get back to a normal life, but I didn't want her to have to take care of me. It just didn't make sense. Nine times out of ten, it was going to keep us in a state of financial worry and tension, and I wanted her and me to walk down a road of prosperity. We didn't need to start our life together standing in a field of quicksand.

Finding a job was way harder than I expected. There were all kinds of openings at the fast-food places where I submitted applications. But nobody would hire me, and I knew it was because of my criminal record. It wasn't like I was underqualified to flip burgers or mop the fucking floor. No, I was being outright discriminated against, and I couldn't even get hired at the KFC Carol managed. She tried to hire me, but her supervisor stopped the process. I tried to stay optimistic, and I kept turning in applications.

It was June 14, 2000, about 10:00 a.m., when Carol picked me up in front of the halfway house and took me back to her apartment. Normally, we'd walk though the door and into the bedroom, get undressed, and have sex, but that day I was thinking about Mario. In two hours he was scheduled to be put to death by the state of Ohio for a crime he didn't commit. His story was finally being covered by the local media and some national media too, and as soon as we got inside I turned on the TV.

"This shit is crazy," I said to nobody as I switched from station to station.

"What's crazy?" Carol asked from across the living room.

I pointed at the TV with the remote and turned toward her. "All three stations all of a sudden are ready to talk about Mario's case. They should have been covering it years ago."

"Yeah. " She let out a sigh. "You think he go get a stay though?"

"Hard to predict what these sleazy politicians go do. The governor should have stepped in on Mario's case a long time ago. But I don't just fault him for being a coward. I'm madder, really, at these weak Black leaders. They sit back and don't do nothing but sing stupid-ass Negro spirituals all damn day."

Carol looked surprised. "My mother sing those songs, boy. Don't talk about them people like that, Malcolm."

"I'm dead serious. If it was the 1960's, you might have some people still singing, but you'd have the militants like Malcolm X and Fred Hampton out there raising hell. Today you don't see anybody putting it down that way. It's like niggas just said 'fuck everything,' or they let that never ending supply of American wool get pulled over their eyes."

We sat in the living room talking about America's Black leadership and Mario's case until the noon news came on. I was hoping to hear some breaking news about a stay of execution by the governor, but the lead anchor, an older White guy, began the broadcast by reporting that just two minutes earlier the governor had denied Mario's request for a stay of execution. I jumped up and shouted *fuck* at the top of my lungs, startling Carol. She jumped up too and gave me a hug, trying to calm me down.

"Say a prayer with me, baby," she said very softly, as she held her arms around my waist and stared into my eyes. She knew I didn't believe in God. But something about her gentle beauty made me want to do it.

"Okay," I said, "and I'm only doing it for the sake of Mario." But I was thinking too about the love I still felt for his beautiful, dead sister, Kandi.

After we finished praying, we sat on the couch and waited for more news about Mario. At 12:21 p.m. the station cut away from a food segment to a live video feed of a middle aged Black female anchor standing outside the entrance to Southern Ohio Correctional Facility in Lucasville, where they housed the death row. "In Lucasville this is Racine Sterling reporting for Action News," she said. "We've just learned that convicted child murderer and rapist Mario Ernesto Sanchez died by lethal injection. The time of his death. . . ."

My mind went blank. I couldn't believe nobody intervened. They just let him die like he was a stray dog. I should have known President Clinton's lying ass wasn't go step up to the plate. In the first six years he was in office over 300 people were executed, over 100 more than the combined total of Bush and Reagan over twelve years. Like Ice Cube said in the rap verse on legendary rapper Scarface's hit album *The Diary*, "Fuck Bill and Hillary!"

When I snapped out of it, I seen Carol was crying, and I gave her a hug. Neither one of us said anything. She seemed distraught, and I was mad. All the bitterness from my time in prison came pouring back inside me, and I kept thinking Mario had been *murdered* by the state for something he didn't do. But even in the midst of my anger, I realized I was getting better at controlling it than when I was in prison. Maybe it was Carol's influence.

After while she let go of me, stepped back, and broke the silence. "Baby," she said softly, "I didn't mean to get so emotional. I just—"

"Hold on," I cut her off. "You don't have to apologize to me for getting *emotional.* As long as I'm your man and we're together, don't ever think you can't cry on my shoulder when something hurts you. I'm not go do you like that last chump did you. I know you ain't used to seeing me mad. But I'm here for you. And I don't play about that *love* word, ever. I just been on edge because of Mario's execution—"

"Baby, you don't gotta explain yourself. I know you love me." Carol grabbed my hand. "I need to stop being so insecure. But I still can't believe they killed your friend. Stevie Wonder or Ray Charles could see he was innocent."

I hadn't gotten drunk since I went to prison, but after Mario's execution, I wanted to get plastered, and I asked Carol to take me to the liquor store for a cheap bottle of E&J. She refused to help me violate the terms of my parole. She knew I needed to unstress myself, though, so she gave me one of the greatest stress relievers known to man. So much for not having sex on my mind!

The morning after Mario's execution everybody and their mama—from the NAACP to professional athletes—was on the radio or TV yelling about it. As I sat in the living room of the halfway house and listened to everybody talk about the tragedy, I got angry again. Not one of them used their celebrity or their political power to help Mario when he was alive. Now they all had something to say about him being wrongfully convicted and executed. It seemed like they were using him to get into the spotlight. After I watched the morning news for a while, I went back to my room and wrote an overdue letter to my surrogate uncle, Deathrow:

June 15, 2000

Dear Uncle Row,

Before I get off into this letter, let me start by apologizing for taking so long to get back with you. I should have wrote, like, a month ago. Things have been a little hectic because I can't get a job. I thought I would have had a job by now. These bastards out here, though, they are some discriminating sons-of-bitches. I can't even get McDonalds to hire me. But enough about me for now.

I know you're pissed off just like me about Mario getting executed. I thought he was go get spared some kind of way. But didn't none of these crooked politicians come to his defense. You'd think at least one of these elected clowns would have been raising hell. But they didn't do shit. And what's crazy, now that I think about it, is every year on Thankstaking holiday the President pardons a turkey! You mean to tell me Clinton's lying ass couldn't spare Mario's life?

I'm go send you some more pictures of me and Carol. I'll have some in the mail for you by next week. I'm go get you some more of those nude ones too. Just don't give yourself a heart attack when you get them. Let me know when you getting out of that lock-up bullshit too. Hopefully, I'll be better situated by the time you get out, and I'll be able to get you a food box.

You got to get up out there though, unc. You too old to be in that madness anyhow, you feel me?

I'm about to wrap this letter up. Carol go be picking me up here shortly so I'm go let you go, unc. You take care of yourself in there. And pour some out for Mario, too!

Peace and Love.

Ya' Nephew,
Malcolm

After I finished writing to Deathrow I felt much better mentally than I did when I first woke up. He had always been an uplifting presence in my life when we were neighbors in the joint. Reminiscing on the good times we had and the insights he shared with me about life, it boosted my spirits and reminded me to stay optimistic about my future.

Despite Mario's execution and even though I couldn't find a job, I had to stay focused.

Chapter Thirty-Five

Throughout the week after Mario's execution, I kept up my job hunting and spent time with Carol. A plastic manufacturing company announced they were seeking to hire 50 ex-offenders, and I turned in my application. My intuition told me the tide was ready to turn.

A couple of days later, I got an answer from Deathrow that confirmed my intuition:

6/21/2000

Nephew!

I figured I was going to hear from you after what they did to Mario. It's a damn shame they killed that boy. That damn Governor we got ain't worth a rat's ass. It's a done deal now, but I wish the boy wouldn't have done what he did.

I see you are going through some rough times. After doing some thinking, I decided to do something about it. I never told you this, and I'll explain why in a minute, but I got a nice chunk of money on my account from when I was in the service. They paid a bunch of us for all that damn Agent Orange they sprayed, plus I get a check every month for my disability. You should be getting a check in the mail in a few days, as soon as it gets processed by the cashier. It's for $10,000. That sounds like a lot, but I get my checks and I got plenty.

The reason I never mentioned the money was because two fools tried to extort me, and I didn't trust anybody after that. The first fool was one of those damned AB's. Some kind of way he found out about my case and tried to tell me he was related to my wife, and then he told me I had to pay him if I wanted to walk on the compound. Listen here, nephew—I started to get me a hawk that day and stab the hell out of that simple bastard. He was too big for me though, nephew. But I didn't give him one red cent. I told this one big young Black fella I worked with what went down, and he pulled down on the AB boy. He put a stop to everything. I gave him a carton of Newports for looking out for me, and when I went to the store, I would grab him a couple of items if he needed something. Well, he wasn't satisfied with that, and he turned around and tried to extort me too. Fucked me up, nephew. I said the hell with everything after that, and I got myself locked up with a small hawk I made. I didn't tell on anybody though—just left the shank on my bed when I went to work. That's why I'm in AC right now. I told them I wasn't going back to population until they send me to the old folks prison in Lima. Warden said they go try to get me up there at the end of the year. I just want to be at peace and relax, nephew. Ain't no spring chicken. Too old to be dealing with these young fools.

Ain't go keep you too long, but write me right away when you get that check. Don't blow it either! Use it for something good. You are a good person with a good head on your shoulders. So use the money wisely. Buy something nice for that pretty gal of yours too.

Take care, nephew.

Lots of Love,
Uncle Row

I had mixed emotions when I finished Deathrow's letter. Naturally, I was shocked and happy he was sending me $10,000! But I hated to hear he had to resort to getting purposely caught with a shank so he could hide out in AC. He was up in age so he probably did the right thing checking into AC. The parasites who knew he had the money weren't go stop trying to extort him. There's no such thing as a bully having mercy in prison. Nine times out of ten, Deathrow ends up seriously hurt or getting extorted out of all his money.

It was late in the evening when I read Deathrow's letter, and I wanted to call Carol and let her know the good news. But she had went straight to work after dropping me off, and I couldn't call until the next morning bright and early.

"Baby, why you calling so early." She sounded groggy. "You not in any trouble, are you?"

"No trouble, sleepy head. I got something to tell you that *you are not go believe*."

"It better be good, calling me collect like this."

I laughed. "Listen, I got a letter from my Uncle Row, and he told me he sent me *ten thousand dollars!*"

"Baby, are you serious?"

I laughed again. "Yeah, I'm serious. I'm go let you read this letter as soon as you get here."

"Oh my God, baby! Where'd he get all that money?"

"He say it's from when he was in Vietnam. He got messed up by that chemical they was spraying. Plus, he get a check every month for being shot. I ain't know he was getting them checks. All he ever told me was he shot his self on purpose to get out of Vietnam."

"When do you think you'll get the money?"

"It takes a few days to process the check, but he said I should get it in a couple more days counting yesterday."

Carol was silent for quite a while. "Then what?" she finally asked. "What you go do with it?"

"Good question," I said slowly. "I stayed up late thinking about it and couldn't really come up with that much. . . . What you think of us starting our own business together?"

"What kind of business?"

"Maybe one of them SMC mail order businesses. They be advertising all the time on them infomercials. You know what I'm talking about?"

"I know *exactly* what you're talking about," Carol said. "Baby, I seen them infomercials, like, a thousand times. That's something we could definitely do. . . . Matter of fact, after I pick you up today, I'm go buy that new monitor for my computer, and then I'm go get online and have SMC send us some brochures on how to get started."

Two days later I got the $10,000 check in certified mail. I didn't tell anybody at the halfway house, but I was so glad to get the check that I ordered pizza for everybody. I called Carol before she went to work and told her the money had arrived. The next day she drove me to the bank, where I deposited $9,500 of the check into my depleted savings account.

After we left the bank, Carol drove me downtown to my PO's office so I could tell him about the money. She hadn't met Mr. Schubert so I asked her to come in with me while I told him. He didn't believe a word!

I should have known he'd be suspicious. Ex-cons don't get $10,000 out of the blue. He had lots of questions, and after a while he called the CCI prison and talked to one of the unit managers about Deathrow. The manager corroborated my story.

I knew everything was okay when a big grin lit up my PO's face. "Well, Mr. Jordan, all is well that ends well."

I smiled and nodded and looked over at Carol, whose face was expressionless. I wanted some kind of way to put a smile on that beautiful face. "Before we leave, Mr. Schubert," I said, grinning at my PO, "I got one more thing to run by you."

He leaned back in his leather office chair and looked down at his watch. "Okay, but it's got to be quick so I can get some lunch."

"It's just a question I want to ask, Mr. Schubert," I said, feeling kind of nervous all of a sudden. "I've been thinking about this for a while, and I want to know if—if I can move out of the halfway house and move in with Carol, this beautiful woman standing next to me here?"

Before he could say a word, Carol blurted out, "Oh, my God!" She was smiling now. "You serious about this, Malcolm?"

"Yeah, I'm serious," I said. "As long as the guy behind the desk says it's okay."

She grabbed me in a hug and gave me a kiss. "Baby," she said softly, "I love you."

"I love you too," I said, looking into her eyes.

Mr. Schubert laughed. "Look at you two lovebirds," he said as he folded his arms across his belly. "And I don't have a problem with you moving out of the halfway house. Shit, Jordan, you've kept your nose clean. . . .It's go take a month for me to complete the process so you can move. I gotta visit your new place of residence." He looked at Carol. "And I gotta fill out a bunch of paperwork. I'll let you know something next week though."

After I was tentatively approved to move out of the halfway house, my good fortune continued. I didn't get hired by the plastic manufacturing company, which surprised me, but the next day I got the word I'd been hired as a dishwasher at a downtown Italian restaurant. I started working at the end of July and shortly after that, my PO gave me the green light to move in with my beautiful Black queen.

Like many young couples living together for the first time, me and Carol spent our first days together having sex, sex, and more sex. Then we got the SMC mail order brochures and started our studying, which included a free online, four-week business start-up seminar. After that I paid $2,500 in start-up fees for color catalog production, website development and advertising, a post office box, and a business license to get our "drop shipping" business started. We called it *Garvey International*, and we sold discount electronic items and clothes that we bought wholesale through our SMC affiliate.

He supplies our merchandise, stocks our inventory, and ships it to our customers for a percentage.

It's almost a year from my release from prison, and I'm working full time from our apartment managing the business. In three months *Garvey International* has netted over $28,000. That's not a huge figure, but $28,000 in three months for a novice entrepreneur just out of prison—that's something!

Who would have thought Malcolm Xavier Jordan, the problem child falsely accused of crimes and an ex-con, would pull his self up by his bootstraps and take all life's lemons thrown at him and turn them into lemon meringue pie?

I never let the flame of hope go out, *refused* to let any negative situation extinguish it, *refused* to let my own bad decisions extinguish it, *refused* to let my time in prison for crimes I didn't commit extinguish it. I *refused* to quit on myself, *refused* to lose.

Trying out for the George Junior Republic basketball team, I learned years ago the difference between winning and losing is *a state of mind.* Winning is a mentality. And losing? As George Junior Republic's Coach Flynt once ferociously yelled at me, sounding like a pissed off Samuel L. Jackson, "Losing is not an option!"

And for me it never will be.

Author's Afterword

Most of the struggles experienced by Malcolm Xavier Jordan are based on my life as an African-American male growing up in Cleveland, Ohio, during the crime-escalating era of the 1980's and 1990's. Like Malcolm, I lived in a dysfunctional household, as well as group homes, reform schools, and foster care. I too was wrongfully convicted for one of the several offenses that sent me to prison in 1994, entering the diabolical Ohio Department of Rehabilitation and Correction as an 18-year-old. ***Brother of The Struggle*** *is a veiled version of my life so far and an attempt to imagine my future.*

Like Malcolm's childhood, mine was emotionally painful and nomadic. I've never met my father or seen a picture of him, and my mother, who grew up in foster care after her mother was murdered, was a cocaine addict. (A photograph of my mother is available at my website, FreeJasonGoudlock.org.) In the early 1980's, after my mother met an older, financially stable man, she moved both of us in with him, and soon afterwards they got married. Not long after this, though, the man who was now legally my stepfather became physically abusive towards my mother and me. Around 1986, when I was ten or eleven, I grew tired of getting beaten and climbed on top of the garage at the home of my surrogate grandparents, James and Bernice Boozer, to whom this novel is dedicated. When I refused to come down and return to my abusive home, I was committed, like Malcolm, to a children's mental health ward. Then, also like Malcolm, I was sent to a Pennsylvania behavioral school, George Junior Republic in Grove City. I lived there for almost three years.

During most of my time at George Junior Republic I was under some kind of disciplinary sanction and forcibly medicated with an anti-depressant, and often I was kept in isolation. Despite being young, I resisted being medicated because it seemed to me I just missed my mother.

After Malcolm is discharged from George Junior Republic in ***Brother of The Struggle*** *there are some events taken from my imagination instead of my life. Events connected to Malcolm's drug dealing with his childhood friend, Pernell, are pure fiction. But Malcolm's illicit relationship with a female employee of his independent living program is based in reality. Malcolm's undisciplined attempt to become a collegiate basketball player is also based on my experience. One of my biggest regrets is that I squandered my chance to go to college and play basketball, an opportunity to make a college roster as a walk-on. My regret is painful today partly because as a 41-year-old prisoner I can still make a two-handed, double-pump reverse dunk!*

The part of the novel where Malcolm is swayed into pleading guilty to crimes he didn't commit is based on my having been pressed by a court-appointed attorney to plead guilty to the aggravated robbery of a donut shop I didn't rob. But while Malcolm's guilty pleading resulted in his being wrongfully convicted for all of his alleged crimes, my guilty pleading resulted in my being wrongfully convicted for just one of the several crimes for which I was justly charged and convicted. In addition to the wrongful conviction for the donut shop robbery, I was convicted of four charges of aggravated robbery and two charges of felonious assault. In 2015 the Ohio Wrongful Conviction Project accepted my case for review. At the time of this writing, they are still investigating my claim of innocence for the donut shop robbery.

During Malcolm's years in prison, many of the jarring events he experiences are similar to mine. Like Malcolm's, my mother died of a drug overdose when I was a prisoner, and I was denied the opportunity to attend her funeral in 1998.

Malcolm is taken aback by seeing White correction officers with Nazi tattoos, and I saw the same thing when I arrived at the Southern Ohio Correctional Facility (SOCF) in 1995. It was a very hostile time for prisoners confined at SOCF because of the eleven-day prison uprising there in 1993. Of the nine prisons where I've been confined since 1994, SOCF is the most racist, with the Lebanon Correctional Facility a close second.

The anger Malcolm experiences when the Ohio Parole Board gives him a sentence continuance he does not believe he deserves is the way I've felt and am currently feeling as I write these words. Like Malcolm, I was sentenced to an indefinite prison sentence. Mine was for six-to-25 years with a nine-year firearm sentencing enhancement. This sentence requires me to go before the Parole Board, which determines whether I can be released from prison. An Ohio law passed in 1996, Senate Bill 2 (SB2) provides definite sentencing guidelines that reduce the length of time an SB2 offender can be made to serve in prison. SB2 offenders do not have to go before the Parole Board to have their release dates determined unless they are serving a life sentence. Unlike people who committed a crime before July 1, 1996, as I did, SB2 offenders serve sentences determined by their trial judges. Because the SB2 sentencing guidelines were not made retroactive, Ohio has institutionalized a sentencing inequality that excessively punishes pre-SB2 prisoners like me.

As a first-time offender, I have now been imprisoned for nearly 23 consecutive years. If I had been sentenced under the less punitive SB2 guidelines, the maximum sentence I could have received would be 19 years. And because I speak out against the injustice within Ohio's criminal justice system, calling attention to verifiable acts of corruption and officer brutality and racism, the Ohio Parole Board in October of 2014 issued an unconscionable sentence continuance of 5 years! At the time of this writing a documentary film, *tentatively titled **Old-Law Con: The Jason Goudlock Story**, is being produced by award-winning New York filmmaker Samuel Crow. A video trailer for the film, as well as updates on my predicament, can be viewed at FreeJasonGoudlock.org.*

*In addition to calling attention in **Brother of The Struggle** to the harrowing circumstances faced by African-American prisoners in Ohio, I highlight the importance of abolishing the death penalty. Former condemned prisoner Arthur "Deathrow" Manningham and wrongfully convicted Mario Sanchez are characters I constructed from the lives of prisoners I came to know during my years at the Ohio State Penitentiary, Ohio's "supermax." Bomani Shakur, one of these prisoners, was known as Keith La Mar when he wrote a memoir, **Condemned: The Whole Story**, about his conviction for committing aggravated murder during the 1993 Lucasville uprising. The book convinced me of his innocence. I was able to read Condemned before it was made generally available.*

*Shakur's innocence claim is particularly convincing when he tells how the state of Ohio's case against him was constructed of fantastical testimony from prisoners who had been coerced and prepped for the witness stand. One witness asserted that the government had implanted computer chips to control him! It is hard to imagine how reasonable doubt could not have been apparent in Shakur's trial. The fact that he could very well be executed, barring a favorable post-conviction ruling, shows why the death penalty must be abolished as an immoral, racist, and class-based machinery of death. Although the execution of the innocent Mario Sanchez in **Brother of The Struggle** is a fictional atrocity, the executions of innocent people in the United States are dark realities.*

*After **Brother of The Struggle**'s Malcolm Xavier Jordan is paroled from prison to a Cleveland halfway house, the success and happiness he attains is part of the post-*

incarceration outcome I imagine for myself. My entrepreneurial aspirations, however, are more ambitious than Malcolm's. I long to succeed in book publishing, online mail order business, automobile restoration, and music and film production, hoping to invest the profits from my business in philanthropic activities such as building scholarship funds for at-risk youth and expanding micro-financing programs that support small-scale agriculture in developing countries. Although the Ohio Parole Board has yet to give me the opportunity to become the redemptive, successful person I aspire to be, I hope readers will view this novel as tangible proof of my readiness and ability to live a productive life in society.

When young African-Americans are being disproportionately incarcerated in juvenile and adult prisons throughout the United States and brutally murdered by one another, as well as by a minority of rogue law enforcement officers, I hope Brother of The Struggle reveals some ways our society can mend the torn fabric of social justice and build true equality. I firmly believe the inhabitants of urban African-American communities like the one I remember in Cleveland can learn practical ways to make us strong. As legendary rapper and scholar KRS-One has belted this out through his career: Knowledge is the key! It was the key that enabled once-upon-a-time miscreant Malcolm Little to shed his criminal past and evolve above racism into the iconic human rights leader Malcolm X. It was the key that enabled a man named Barack Obama to become the first African-American President of the United States. (But I should admit I don't agree with all of President Obama's policies.) And it was the key that enabled me to write this novel, which I hope you have enjoyed reading and will share with others.

Jason Goudlock
Author, Visionary, and a Brother of The Struggle